PASSIONATE ALIEN

SIR PATRICK BIJOU

BOOK DESCRIPTION

It's not every day that beings from different planets collide. But when they do, a celestial kind of lust emerges, leaving humans and aliens drooling for more.

When Kayleigh Griffin started her job, the last thing she expects is to come face to face with the inhabitants of the cosmic bodies she and her peers have been dutifully studying.

But that certainly was the case one night when a rebel alien decided to make contact. Kayleigh can't believe what she is hearing.

Quickly phoning her mentor Richard, her excitement is met with his healthy scepticism as they decide to investigate further the next day.

With that out of the way, Kayleigh and her boyfriend Tom — whose only intention was to hand-deliver a tasty snack for his girl in her office — erupt in sweet lovemaking, bursting with excitement over the life-changing alien phenomenon and their lust for each other.

However, the thrills don't stop there.

Still recovering from their steamy coupling, the duo step outside to investigate a peculiar light peering from the windows... only to discover that this would be the last time they will see Earth.

With their alien abductors willing to give in to their lustful fancies, Kayleigh, Tom, and another Earthling slowly watch their unwillingness melt away into a grand, titillating adventure into extraterrestrial pleasures.

"Passionate Alien" by Sir Patrick Bijou is another scintillating erotic, sci-fi adventure filled with kinky alien sex and even more carnal explorations that no man has ever experienced.

If you're looking for a captivating read that will heat your cold, lonely nights, get ready to meet your next favourite erotica series.

ABOUT THE AUTHOR

Sir Patrick Bijou lives and writes from the United Kingdom and is the author of several books on finance and fiction. He is known for his extraordinary skills in settling and negotiating peace settlements and international law and is a prodigious legal and political adviser. His diverse writing ability has been influenced by many experiences, making him the success he is today.

Sir Patrick has written many books and articles about the liberation of people, highlighting the issues of those whom the literary world of creative writing has not enlightened. His expedition into content writing has made him a remarkably inspired author and professional communicator.

He has written over 32 non-fictional and fictional books spanning different genres.

Finding his Books.

To find out more about Sir Patrick, visit his website.

www.sirpatrickbijou.com
www.bijouebook.com

Table of Contents

Chapter: 1

Kayleigh had first fallen in love with the stars when she was eight. It was the annual summer vacation up north, into the soft-focus land of cottages and evergreens, where they all relaxed in the slow summer cool and Kayleigh tried to ignore the impending school year. But this time her mother had been replaced by her father's new girlfriend, a spindly thing that seemed to have walked out of a clothes ad, and her father never left her alone -- since this was his monthly weekend, he wanted to make up for the lost time. Everything was indescribably off.

But that night, as she lay on the grass listening to cicadas in the distance, she looked up at the stars and was suddenly filled with an intoxicating mixture of calm and wonder. It was nothing like the city, where only one or two brave lights poked out from behind the cloak of smog and light pollution. There were so many stars, uncountable, all spread out before her but always out of her reach. Unlike her rapidly mutating family, the stars were eternal, and always reliable.

There would be more nights at the cottage, and plenty more stargazing, but it was that night more than anything else that brought Kayleigh to where she was today.

Where she was today was in her university's astronomy lab at 1:13 AM, gazing into a telescope with extreme boredom. This was typical grad student minion work. Twice a week she had to spend her nights watching the skies for signs of anomalies, whatever that meant. So far everything had been peaceful every night, and the same stars that used to produce such wonder for her had become a dull duty of employment. One of the other grad students had claimed to have seen a star go supernova on his watch, but other than that everyone agreed that it was a dull burden.

There was a knock at the door, startling Kayleigh out of her self-pitying reverie. She wondered who it could be at this hour -- security wondering why the lights were on, or perhaps something more ominous.

It turned out to be something significantly less ominous. Tom, her boyfriend, waved at her through the little window inside the door. She let him in. "What are you doing up this late?"

"Horror movie marathon on the TV," said Tom. "And then I figured since I was already up and too scared to sleep, I might as well bring you a little care package." He handed her a mass of tin foil, inside which was wrapped a couple of cookies and a BLT sandwich.

"Aw, my favorite," said Kayleigh, taking a bite of the cold sandwich. "You're such a sweetie." She kissed him on the cheek, leaving a ring of bacon grease in her wake.

He blushed in that cute way he always did and jabbed his fingers together. "Well, it was nothing you know... you're the one who's out here doing science and everything."

Kayleigh had met Tom at a campus pub, instantly attracted to him because he was the only one who looked as out of place and uncomfortable as she felt. He had turned out to be a nice guy, although more than a little childish, with his bedroom full of sci-fi books and toys. Nowadays she felt sorry for him more than anything else. After college, he had failed to find a job in the toilet-bowl economy and unlike Kayleigh hadn't had the foresight to hide in academia. She had toted him off like a pet to this big research university halfway across the country, where he spent his days watching soap operas and trying to figure out how far her stipend could stretch.

All that, and she wasn't even faithful to him.

It was one time, Kayleigh kept trying to tell herself. Everyone failed to live up to their morals once in a while. ("Failed to live up to her morals" sounded a lot better in her head than "fucked her supervisor at a conference".) But every day she mentally repeated her infidelity in her mind. The feel of Richard's curly chest hair against her cheek, his masculine musk, the soft head of his uncut cock... she couldn't forget a second of it. She and Richard hadn't spoken about it since returning from that fateful conference, but deep down she knew that if the opportunity came up she would do it again.

"Kay?" said Tom, waving his hand in front of her face. "You listening?"

"What?" She had been distracted by the strain of pity and guilt that had been a constant presence in her mind for the past three months. "Oh, sorry. I just zoned out for a second there. Late night."

"You sure you're okay to work like this?"

She waved away the concern. "If I get too tired I'll just grab a Coke from down the hall. That machine has to have like fifty bucks in quarters from me alone in it."

"I think there's like a 24-hour coffee place around here. If you want I can get you some java from there."

Kayleigh couldn't help but smile. Sometimes she felt like a big sister to Tom, which was sweet but not really conducive to a romantic relationship. "It's okay. For the last time, you don't have to wait on me."

"You're right," he said. Tom glanced at the display monitors, full of anonymous stars and data he couldn't comprehend. "I guess I should be going then."

"Well, I never said you had to go," she said, laying her hand on his. "I wouldn't mind some company on this long dark night."

Ten minutes later they were making out, him straddling her on the leather office chair which somehow managed not to collapse under both their weights. The feeling of Tom's tongue in her mouth and his hands running up and down her sides was nice, Kayleigh thought. The fear of getting caught made it almost nostalgic. It felt like high school. But there, again, was the issue: it seemed like a stupid thing to complain about, but things were too comfortable with Tom, too familiar.

A loud buzz interrupted them. It was the radio, the powerful receiver steered towards the stars. With a guilty look on her face, Kayleigh pulled herself away from her boyfriend and flipped the switch to open a radio channel. "Hello?"

There was a lot of static. Kayleigh frowned and moved to hang up, but suddenly a voice broke through. It was bizarre, like an accent neither of them had ever heard before, in an androgynous voice. Even the basic sounds were off, simple vowels tripped over. But for all that, the message was still quite comprehensible.

"Greetings to the denizens of Ira-3... the planet you call Earth... my name is Gaog, and I am not supposed to be contacting you."

Kayleigh flipped on the transmitter. "Who is this? Is this a prank?"

"But I must tell you... there are worlds and species out there beyond compare. Species are just as intelligent, if not more, than you. They do not want to deal with you. They think you are too primitive, too destructive. But I believe differently."

"I'm asking you again... who is this?"

The speaker didn't respond to their words, just continued on. "Do not destroy yourselves. We are watching, and if you just hold on for a little longer, manage to pull back from the brink... all will be yours, and you shall be introduced into the society of the universe."

Kayleigh and Tom exchanged looks of bafflement. She ran her hands over the controls at lightning speed. There was a long patch of static, and then the voice continued.

"If you heed nothing else I say, heed this... you are not alone."

The transmission cut off as abruptly as it had begun. "Hello? Are you still there?" Kayleigh frantically tried to trace the transmission, trying every method she knew to determine its origin. And then, eventually, one worked.

She took in a deep breath. "It wasn't a prank."

"What do you mean?"

"That transmission came from the orbit of Mars."

Tom still looked perplexed. "So, was it like astronauts dicking around or something?"

"There are no astronauts around fucking Mars Tom." Kayleigh's voice was not angry but excited, almost giddy. Scratch that, absolutely giddy. "This is the real deal. A genuine, bonafide, real-life alien transmission. Holy shit."

"You sure?" Tom asked. By this time his girlfriend was bounding around the lab, manic glee filling every pore of her body. She punched the air vigorously and then skipped around the huge telescope in the center of the room.

"Pretty damn sure." She bounded back into her seat, though her excitement would not be denied, and the energy transferred itself to twitching fingers and a stomping foot. "We need to send a reply. I need to notify people... God, can you wrap your head around it? An actual alien is talking to us."

Tom still had a look of disbelief on his face. Kayleigh guessed he was right to be skeptical -- this was pretty fantastical after all, and it could still be just a well-executed prank. But it didn't feel like it. She had a hunch that this was real, that this transmission was the big one.

The alien had used English, so that was what she decided to reply to. Kayleigh grabbed the old dusty radio set and promptly began transmitting. "We have received your message. My name is Kayleigh Griffin, and I am... a scientist. We want to learn about these worlds that you speak of. Who are you? What are you? Please reply."

Silence reigned in the observatory. Kayleigh was half out of her seat, leaning forward on her haunches, waiting tensely for the next transmission. Tom still seemed dumbfounded. "Of all the nights for me to bring food..." he said under his breath, then shook his head and went back to quiet.

They waited. And waited. But the deafening radio silence persisted.

Kayleigh cast a glance towards the clock. An hour had passed. It had certainly seemed like a long time, but it still struck her. Had something happened to their contact? Had he (or she or it or some pronoun humans couldn't even comprehend) only intended to send the one short message, and would leave them in the dark, trying to decipher those few lines? Had her message failed in whatever way? Would she be known as the incompetent grad student that ruined the first contact?

"I need to call Richard... I mean, Professor Bell." She got up from her seat and paced around the room, anxiously jabbing numbers into her cell phone. It was 3 AM, but she knew that Richard would want to hear the news as soon as possible. Honestly, she should have called him an hour ago.

The phone rang three times before she heard that ragged, sexy voice. How could she think about sex, especially infidelity, at a time like this, she chided herself. "Kay, you'd better have a damn good reason for waking me up in the middle of the night."

"I do." And then the whole story came out in excited childish ramblings. Kayleigh wished she could see Richard's face and take in his reaction. Over the phone he was silent, giving her nothing but the occasional heavy breath, and she had no idea whether he believed her or not.

Finally, after she had exhausted herself, he spoke. "Are you sure about this? Have you triple-checked the coordinates?"

"Quadruple checked them. This is too exciting to fuck up."

He was chuckling in that parental way he did. "Well, it might be a problem with the machine. Let's wait until tomorrow and I'll check to make sure it's working properly. If it is... then we have quite the discovery on our hands."

"Great." She was beaming. "I'll see you tomorrow then."

"Don't get too wound up -- as I said, it's probably just a glitch. Still... don't tell anyone else, okay? Department secret, for now."

"Uh huh." After a few more pleasantries she hung up. The manic energy of discovery, of having a childhood fancy appear before her practically wrapped in a bow, was still filling Kayleigh. She wanted to go dancing, run a marathon, or get in a big fight. But she couldn't abandon her post.

She bounded up to Tom, who was watching the screen, waiting for something to happen again. It seemed like he might be waiting a long time. She threw her arms around him and gave him a big sloppy kiss. "Let's fuck!"

"Wait, are you serious?"

"I'm always serious about fucking." She was nibbling his neck and unbuttoning his shirt. "We're probably the only two people on campus. We can make as much noise as we want."

Tom's resistance, never too well built up in the first place, was rapidly crumbling. "But... where..."

Kayleigh looked around at the numerous desks. She found one with nothing fragile on it and swept all the papers and books aside. "I've always wanted to do that." She whipped off her shirt and tossed it away. It landed on the edge of a cubicle, where it continued to hang. Kayleigh lay down on the desk and began working out of her jeans. She was wearing simple black underwear underneath -- nothing frilly, but alluring nonetheless. Truth be told, a body like hers didn't need much in the way of packaging.

Tom looked nervous, although a tent in his slacks betrayed his attraction. "Are you sure there isn't a camera going or something?"

"Todd, I am getting fucked right now, and if you aren't up for it then I'm just going to have to lay here and fuck myself."

He still looked hesitant, so she made good on her threat. She slipped two fingers into her panties and ran them along her puffed-up pussy lips. Even she was surprised at how wet she was. She inched her panties down her stickiness, then let them slide down her legs, revealing her patch of brown pubic hair and the glistening slit underneath. She ran her hands along her entrance and tossed her long hair back, trying to do the best imitation of a porno magazine for the dumbfounded-looking Tom.

Secretly she was a bit of an exhibitionist. Maybe it made her a slut, but Kayleigh loved the feeling of mastery that came when a man's attention was firmly and totally fixed on her. She and Todd loved to masturbate for each other, although they never had the willpower to stick with it -halfway through they would break off from their solitary pursuits and be all over each other.

It looked like that would be the case here, with the naughty setting of a scientific building you were definitely not supposed to fuck in increasing the rush. Tom's pants were around his ankles, and he was stroking his already stiff cock, looking vaguely hypnotized. Kayleigh slid a finger inside her cunt, and the sensation shocked her. Somehow being penetrated made the whole insane situation feel more real. She made a come-hither motion and Tom began slowly shuffling towards her, the tip of his cock gleaming with precum.

And then he tripped over the pants that still clung to his ankles and stumbled until he fell down onto the table, spread halfway across his girlfriend, inadvertently headbutting her belly button. There was a brief pause, and then both burst out laughing.

"Smooth move, Romeo," said Kayleigh in between giggles.

"You distracted me with sexiness," Tom muttered into her belly.

"I think I might have bruised ribs or something."

Tom looked up with a wicked grin. "Awww. You want me to kiss your boo-boo?"

Without waiting for a reply, Tom leaned down and left a hot kiss on her stomach, followed by a long lick of his tongue that sent a compulsive shiver through Kayleigh. He didn't linger on the allegedly injured area for long, though, instead working his way down to the hot and wet delta between her thighs.

Tom laid a kiss on her nether lips and Kayleigh squirmed. His practiced tongue slid out and flicked ever so lightly against her cunt and hard clit. She grabbed him by his shoulder-length brown hair and tried to forcefully shove him deeper into her sex. She was not in the mood for being teased tonight.

He obliged with a more forceful ravaging of her pussy, tongue sliding hard between her lower lips and bathing her wet gap in a sheen of saliva. Kayleigh threw back her head and moaned as she felt ripples of pleasure emanate from her most sensitive areas. Tom had learned exactly what made her scream and was doing it all tonight. But still, it wasn't enough.

Kayleigh grabbed him by the hair again and pulled him up. "Enough," she said, her voice surprising her with its huskiness. "Fuck me. Fuck me as hard as you possibly can."

A second later she felt the slam of his cock forcefully entering her. Tom didn't have the biggest cock she'd ever seen, but it seemed custom-made for her, fitting smoothly into her pussy and shaped just right to hit those spots that consistently sent her into spasms of ecstasy. Tonight was no different. As she felt his girth fill her, she let out a sigh of absolute contentment, already feeling her cunt buzzing in anticipation.

Tom pulled Kayleigh to the edge of the desk and pushed her legs up, giving him the angle to fuck her deeper. And then he was thrusting away, his hips pumping and driving her into the hardwood beneath her. That impact only gave her another illicit thrill, as strong sensations pulsed from her pussy to the tips of her fingers, with clutched reflexively from the edge of the desk.

He was fucking her with absolute abandon, slamming his cock into her as fast as he could, enjoying the simple animal pleasure of coupling. For her part, Kayleigh was thrusting back as well as she could, trying to capture this fantastic cock and enjoy the sensations it was giving her forever. It didn't take long for both of them to reach the edge. Kayleigh felt the tension building in her torso and knew soon it was going to explode.

"Fuck me!" Her cry was practically a snarl. "I'm gonna come! Oh god, fuck me!"

The orgasm wracked her whole body. She shot up and clutched Tom's back, digging her fingernails into his shirt as her flesh hummed with overwhelming pleasure. She heard him gasp and felt his cock pulsing within her, spilling his hot seed into her quivering cunt.

"Jesus," Kayleigh said a moment later. "That was crazy."

Tom shook his head, awakening from his sex-induced reverie. "Well, it was your idea."

"I know." She hopped off the table. There were no cameras around that she knew of, but their sweat and juices were all over the table, and its carefully arranged papers were in a mess on the floor. As she stood she felt some of Tom's cum drip out of her and onto the laboratory floor.

It was then that she noticed the light outside. Curious and heedless of her state of undress, Kayleigh walked to the window. She couldn't see any obvious source of the brightness, but it was bright as day, although the light was artificial. This inexplicable shine was entrancing. Mites of dust danced in the warm glow, and Kayleigh felt something -- she wasn't sure what, she didn't care -- leaving her body.

Tom was right beside her, naked from the waist down, staring slack-jawed out the window. She held his hand as they stared at the wonderful light.

"We should go outside," Tom said, his voice sounding unusual.

Outside. Of course, they should be outside. Where else could they be, at such a time as this? Everything, everything, would be solved if they only stepped outside.

There was something important that was happening here, that was just going on. Kayleigh couldn't quite remember what it was. Oh well. It could wait. The light was urgent.

Holding hands, she and Tom stepped out into the light. Despite the autumn cold nipping at her privates in the faraway place her senses were, she felt great. For a moment she felt that elusive feeling humans are always chasing and never managing to get a firm grip on -- contentment, belonging, absolute and total satisfaction.

She looked down and found that her bare feet were slowly leaving the ground. She was being pulled up into the sky. Oh well. That was just the kind of thing that happened here. Kayleigh closed her eyes and she fell into something a lot like sleep, but much sweeter.

The heavy cover hugged her like a mother nursing her young. Tom was next to her, wrapped up equally tight. Their fingers were interlaced. Kayleigh liked mornings like this. They could just lay there all morning, indulging in sloth and lust, as she didn't have to go to school in the afternoon-

School. The observatory. The message, which she was audacious enough to believe had genuinely come from the stars.

Kayleigh rolled out of the bed, kicking the covers away, landing on the floor on her hands and knees. She didn't remember coming home last night or going to bed. That wasn't too unusual, but as the numbing tendrils of sleep slowly lost their grip she began to realize that something was distinctly wrong. This wasn't her room. This wasn't any room she had ever been in before.

It was a nice bedroom, to be sure -- bigger than any she had been in, with a four-poster bed, a fancy chest of drawers, a bookshelf stocked with the classics, and other aristocratic furnishings. But it wasn't hers. And the view outside the window was not a ground-level image of their sleepy college town.

"Tom," Kayleigh said quietly. "Why are we in New York?"

It was a skyline she had learned from countless TV shows and movies, looking exactly as it had in the cinema. It was a gorgeous view of a nonsensical one. Tom muttered something monosyllabic and rolled over.

Kayleigh poked him in the chest until he eventually managed to pull himself to a sitting position. Tom shook out his long hair as if some strands of sleep were stuck in it. "What's the big deal, Kay?" And then he took a look around and looked equally baffled.

"Have you ever been here before?" she said.

"Nope. Last I checked we were at your uni, not... here."

"I don't even remember falling asleep," she said.

Both of them sat there for a moment as if hoping that if they waited long enough they would wake up in their beds. Or maybe they were just waiting for something to happen. But nothing did.

It was Kayleigh who got up first. "I guess we should see what's through that door." Tom nodded, looking nervous.

Through the door and down a brief hallway they came to what seemed like a common room, lit by scattered lamps. It seemed as though night had abruptly fallen, as no light came through the window. It looked like it wouldn't be out of place at her university, aping a kind of stuffy English academicism. Sitting on a comfortable-looking armchair with a plate of toast was her graduate advisor, in his boxer shorts.

"Richard?" Kayleigh said. "What are you doing here?"

"Same thing as you, I'd imagine," said Richard. He looked the two of them up and down appraisingly, and it was only then that Kayleigh realized her state of undress. She and Tom were just as they had been after their impulsive coupling on the desk, wearing only a bra and a shirt respectively. She blushed furiously and tried to cover her privates, while Tom tugged his shirt down until it at least halfway covered his twig and berries.

"Oh, there's no need to be shy," Richard said. "I get the feeling that we're going to be here for a while, so we at least ought to be comfortable around each other."

"Where is here?" said Kayleigh, her curiosity momentarily overcoming her self-consciousness.

Richard jerked a finger towards the window. "It took me a while to stop it cycling through famous cityscapes, but I think I've got what is outside now."

Kayleigh and Tom crab-walked over to the window, trying to stay decent, even if Richard was going to have a perfect view of both their asses in a minute. He just took another bite of his toast and looked greatly amused. But when they saw what was out there they both forgot about modesty.

It was space -- littered with stars like the night sky Kayleigh loved, but instead of fading away to the horizon, it kept going, encapsulating them completely. The sun was a glimmering light burning far away. It took them a few minutes to recognize the pale blue disk receding in the background as Earth.

There was a deep, authoritative voice behind them. It didn't sound anything like Richard. "That is your home planet. Take a good look, as you won't be back there."

Chapter: 2

Kayleigh whirled around. Standing behind her was an authoritative-looking man in a suit, clean-shaven and with fading brown hair. He looked like the sort of man who would play the President in a movie. Kayleigh found herself backing up against the window, trying to put distance between her and the sudden arrival.

"This guy just popped up out of the floor," said Richard, as though he was watching TV. "It was pretty crazy."

Tom stepped in front of his girlfriend, trying to look intimidating despite his pantlessness. The man in a suit chuckled. "Don't worry. I mean you no harm. If I did, I would simply drop you into space and be done with it. I have come here to talk."

"Well good, because we need some answers," said Tom.

Kayleigh thought he looked quite adorable when he tried to act tough. She put a hand on his shoulder. "Let's sit down, Tom. Hear what this guy has to say."

The couch was quite comfortable, soft white leather that yielded to their bodies. The man in the suit decided to remain standing. "First off," he said,

"I should like to apologize. We have treated you most unfairly, and while that unfairness is necessary and frankly inevitable, you still have every right to be angry at me."

No response. Even Richard was on edge waiting for his next words.

"Approximately ten of your hours ago, a rebel named Gaog sent out an unauthorized transmission to your planet. Currently, Ide-3 is under consideration for admission to the League of Worlds, and a strict communications blackout has been applied. Gaog was not the first and will not be the last to violate that blackout, but the damage he has done must be minimized. There is a procedure we follow in these cases. The perpetrator is brought to justice in the Galactic Court, and anyone who knows of their message is quarantined from the rest of the population, so to speak."

Kayleigh was trying to figure out the truth behind the man's official-ese. "And by quarantined, you mean... abducted?"

"That is the word often used in popular accounts, yes. They are removed from their home planet and placed under the custody of the League of Worlds."

Richard was up and starting to pace. Kayleigh had noticed this in him before whenever something unusual or interesting would come up in their data. "So what you're saying is that you whisked us up to take us off to space, without so much as a hello, and no matter how we feel about it we can't go back to Earth again?"

"That is a negative way to phrase it, but yes."

Tom had his head in his hands. "Can't you just wipe our memories? Like in that movie..."

"Men in Black?" said the man in the suit.

"Aliens watched that?"

"With great mirth. Memory erasure was the original technique used, but without extensive research requiring human subjects, it was unreliable and tended to cause brain trauma."

"So instead you're just abducting us," said Richard. "Well, that's great. You know, I have friends, people at the university... they're going to notice I'm gone."

The man in the suit remained unemotional. "That's being taken care of. At this point, I'd recommend you stop thinking about it. You're beginning a new life, in a much faster and more advanced world than the one you know. This is an opportunity very few people get, and most everyone who does is glad for it in the end. You will meet alien species, travel to new planets, and enjoy technology you could never have imagined. You are free to explore the galaxy, go wherever you want -- except back to your home."

Kayleigh thought she should have been more distressed about that, but at the moment it was hard to process any of this as real. She thought it might be a dream -- but in a dream, you never think that. Of course, she had spent long nights arguing with friends that aliens had to be out there somewhere -- but deep down she had never really believed it, not as more than an intellectual notion. They existed only on paper, not as something you could reach out and touch. She thought she should say something, ask a question, or yell at their abductor, but she seemed to have lost the ability to combine words into a sentence.

Richard was perched on the edge of his seat with an eager, almost manic look on his face. Kayleigh recognized it from class -- from the rare moments when a student would seem to genuinely get something and show a glimmer of promise. "So, who are you? Another abductee? A human Uncle Tom?"

"My name is not Tom," said the man in a suit. (In the back of her mind Kayleigh was glad because two Toms would just confuse things even more.) "I have been called Wings of Iron, Circler of Long Spaces, He Who Lives In Lockstep... you must understand, my race communicates psychically, through concepts, which may be somewhat unwieldy on the human tongue."

"So you're not human?" Richard stared intently at the man's body as if trying to find an abnormality beneath his clothes.

The man -- Wings of Iron or one of his many long names -- nodded. "I am one of the Erusmi. I have merely taken this form to create something familiar for you -- a voice of authority you would understand."

"Well, it was a nice gesture, I guess," said Tom. "So what do you look like?"

"I am a being of pure energy. I take whatever form I choose." Wings of Iron cast a hand at the floor beneath them. "I am the ship that you are in right now, as well as the humanoid speaking to you, as well as the furniture you are sitting on. My species moved beyond fixed material forms many eons ago."

Tom got off the couch, staring back at it. "You're telling me I was just sitting on you?"

"Don't worry. I'm not offended."

He shivered, looking around, frantic at his inability to not be in contact with this alien creature. Wings of Iron continued. "I can create any kind of item you need."

"Can you make us some clothes?" said Kayleigh, still feeling rather exposed.

"Certainly." The walls shifted again, before spitting out a plain white T-shirt and black sweatpants. Kayleigh tugged them on.

"Um, Kay, you do realize that you're wearing him," said Tom.

Kayleigh shivered but kept the clothes on. "I'm just not gonna think about that. It's better than wandering around in my birthday suit the whole time."

"You know," said Richard. "I have to wonder what you two were doing when you got abducted..." The other two blushed.

Wings of Iron cleared his throat. "Even with space slipping, it will take about two weeks to reach Jian-2, the central planet of the League of Worlds. I understand that this is a lot to take in, but please get comfortable. Make yourselves at home, as you say." And with that, the man in the suit stepped into the wall and promptly melted away.

It took everyone a moment to process the conversation's abrupt end. "Like hell he understands," says Kayleigh. She kicked at the nearest wall, but it felt as hard and unfeeling as any wall did. She clutched her feet and cursed. When she finally quieted down, the room was eerily silent. The usual filter of the city noise was completely absent. It was only in silence that the three realized that they were truly alone.

"So," said Richard. "Anyone sees any good movies lately?"

The first day was a question of survival. Wings of Iron produced items upon request but didn't say anything to them. The first thing they requested was a deck of playing cards, which they used to play poker until they were all sick of it and had won and lost imaginary fortunes many times over.

But they had to eat, eventually. At Richard's suggestion, the three began requesting increasingly elaborate meals from the energy being, beginning with high cuisine pasta and ending with a big turkey dinner that could have fed eight. But the ship just silently complied with everything. The food all looked gorgeous but tasted bland.

Boredom set in quickly. Kayleigh would never think she would get bored so quickly of an alien experience, but there was genuinely nothing to do. Wings of Iron produced a chess set and a go board, but said he couldn't replicate movies or books -- he hadn't spent enough time studying Earth culture. Tom and Richard eventually gave in and asked for clothes, and got the same white shirt and black pants. Whatever Earth culture the alien had imbibed, fashion was not included.

Tom and Kayleigh both slept fitfully when they could sleep at all. They both tossed and kicked in the hotel bed, trying to shake the feeling of being wrapped up in somebody's skin. (She guessed it would be more like someone's internal organs, but declined to follow that train of thought to the end.) Sometimes they would turn over simultaneously, bodies colliding with each other, and smile in shared recognition at each other.

But somehow, in the dim hours of the early morning (according to their watches, at least -- out here there was nothing to differentiate day from night, and their Earthly system of time seemed quaint and artificial) Kayleigh drifted off to sleep. When she woke up, she was crying.

Tom, who seemed to have an instinctive sense of these things, put his arms around her and hugged her tight to his chest. "What's the matter?"

She was thinking about people. Melissa, her best friend since high school, of short hair and shorter temperament, got her through every break-up or other personal tragedy with all-night sessions of alternating between video games and shoulder-crying. Dale, the dorkiest of all her dorky friends, with the big horn-rimmed glasses and the infinite well of jokes. Dr. Jameson, the gray-haired professor who had gone to bat for her and got her this grad school spot, all without so much as a you're-welcome. Her parents were aggravating and embarrassing but ultimately loving. Her little sister, just about to start college, with undecided ambitions but brilliant energy.

And she would never see any of them again.

It hadn't hit her until that moment, in the haze between wakefulness and sleep. "I want to go home," she pleaded into Tom's shirt. "I want to see them again. Just one last time, please?" She wasn't sure who she was pleading with -- her powerless boyfriend, or the seemingly emotionless alien who surrounded them all, whose skin she was truly crying into right now.

She looked up at the ceiling, wondering if and how Wings of Iron would respond. "Look, I'm sorry. I'm just an astronomy geek. I didn't mean to eavesdrop on your intergalactic business or anything. Can you just bring me back home? I promise I won't tell anyone about the message. No one would believe me if I did. So won't you please just bring us back to Earth?"

No response from the ship-alien. Kayleigh banged on the walls, but they were as hard as before. Tom was behind her, holding on as if not to let her drift away, but all she could feel right now was rage and grief.

Richard wasn't mourning anyone that night. Truth be told, he had long since grown sick of dealing with all the sycophants and careerists in his department, and every one of his relationships -- family, friends, lovers -- he had ruined years ago. So why not accept a new life in an alien world? Wasn't that what he had always wanted, tucked away in library stacks throughout his childhood, staring at golden age sci-fi until his eyes strained?

Instead that night he couldn't sleep for the energy, the raw curiosity of it all. Richard suddenly needed to know absolutely everything about this new world he was entering, especially all the strange things that Wings of Iron had referred to casually, as one might mention bread or a mailbox without explaining it.

"Ship guy," he said, tapping on a wall. "Can I ask you some questions?"

A moment later, the wall started bulging before spitting out the same man in a suit that had talked to them earlier. "I don't see why not," said Wings of Iron. "I'll answer them to the best of my ability."

Richard patted the side of the queen-sized bed the ship-alien had provided for him. "Come on up here. Um, can I call you Wing? I need something a little more human-sounding."

"You can call me whatever you want. I'm not going to stop you." The main removed his shoes, which promptly melted into the carpet, and climbed into bed with Richard.

Richard drummed his finger against the sheets. He felt uncomfortable in the extreme. "Sorry, this may sound like a weird request, but... could you be a girl?" He had always felt more comfortable teaching and talking to women. With men, he always thought they were staring at him like a challenge as if even in a classroom they were in some way an adversary or opponent. It was stupid and sexist, he knew, but that was just the way things seemed to him.

Wing blinked and, without so much as a word, began to change (or at least his human extension did.) His body began to narrow and shrink visibly, with his clothes quickly shrinking in time to his new body. Two small breasts emerged from his chest, while he (if he was even the right word) swallowed his Adam's apple with a gulp. The geometry of Wing's face was rearranged, lines and angles shifting, and then suddenly he was a she. A masculine woman, perhaps -- Wing hadn't changed her short hair or officious black suit -- but a woman. Richard realized that his mouth had been hanging open in awe for at least a minute.

"Is this sufficient?" she asked, in a lighter and silkier voice than before.

"Um... yeah. Definitely." Richard cleared his throat. What had he wanted to know again? All he could think of now was whether or not Wing had changed his/her/its/their genitals under that suit, or whether she had even had private parts, to begin with. But asking about that wouldn't be gentlemanly. "So, you've been talking about like a League of Worlds or whatever. Is that who you work for?"

"In essence, yes," said Wing. "Although I should note that 'work' is not how your species describes it. I require no sustenance or material objects, for obvious reasons, so there is no exchange of services for currency, as you are used to. I do this work because I believe in the League's mission."

"Which is snapping up innocent scientists from lesser worlds?"

The wing was unfamiliar with human expressions, but she managed an apologetic look. "If you had suffered through the Voralian Wars, you would understand the importance of building a peaceful interspecies community, and of isolating species that are not ready."

"You're a weird energy being," said Richard. "How much can you suffer?"

Wing got up and looked out the fake window, showing the blank canvas of space. Her human body was tight and tense. "Believe me, the Voralian developed ways... friends of mine died in agony. Make no mistake, the Erusmi can be killed -- and it is the most absolute destruction known to any being."

There was a long pause. Richard whistled. "Damn. Guess I kind of brought the mood down, didn't I?"

"Do not worry. I am here to answer your questions. You should not be afraid of offending me." Wing's face had remained static through the whole exchange, and Richard thought she hadn't got the full suite of human emotions down yet, or rather simply wasn't bothering to emote through her puppet body.

"Okay then." Richard lay on his side, propping his head up with his arm. "So, can you tell me what's keeping Earth from getting into your little club and me from getting a Nobel Prize? I mean, we're not perfect, but I think we humans are a pretty advanced species. You shoulda beamed up my iPhone and I could have shown you what we were capable of."

Wing sat down on the edge of the bed. "In terms of electronic and military technology, yes, humans are quite advanced -- certainly more advanced than some races we've admitted. But in cultural technology, you are quite backward, and this has proved to be a very dangerous combination in the past."

"Cultural technology?" The two words sounded funny together on Richard's tongue.

He thought he could detect the hint of a smile in Wing's staid face. "The fact that you do not even have a concept for it speaks volumes."

"Hey, quit ragging on my species. Sorry, we can't all be mystical energy space-creatures."

"Well, you did ask."

Richard decided to ignore that she was right -- ignoring when other people were right was a vital academic skill, and one he had honed to perfection. Instead, he started looking over the human body she had chosen. Maybe it was just the strangeness of the situation, but he couldn't look away from the stone-faced, borderline androgynous girl. Her style was masculine, but there were two distinctly feminine bulges on her chest and a lithe body under it that he wondered what it would be like to have.

He felt like chiding himself for being so typical. Put in a situation with a literal galaxy's worth of knowledge and discovery at his fingertips, and all he thought about was sex. But Richard supposed that he had plenty of time to learn.

Richard sat up and knelt on the bed behind Wing. He reached out to rub her shoulders. Apparently, in space, this wasn't as played-out a move as it was on Earth. Wing flinched at first, but didn't move away.

"So, can I ask you a personal question?"

"I have already said I will answer everything."

"Great. Well, I guess this is more of a biological thing but does your species... you know, have sex? I imagine it is difficult with the energy thing and all."

If Wing was scandalized, it didn't show in her voice. "Not in our natural forms, no. I have had sex in the form of many different species, however. It is an interesting experience, but also a superficial one, and I don't understand why so many species are fixated on it."

Richard chuckled. He remembered some of his more hopelessly dorky colleagues saying the same thing -- for them it was a case of sour grapes if there ever was one. "Have you ever done it as a human?"

Wing looked at him askew. "No. Do you want to have sex with me?"

"Is that a question or a proposition?" said Richard, putting on his best lady-killer growl.

Wing stood up and changed again. The suit she was wearing seemed to melt into her body, and then disappear, leaving her shamelessly naked before him. Even for Richard, this was a bit more forward than he was used to. "You know," said Wing. "You will find that seduction is a peculiarly human game, one that you don't have to go through with me or many others. Most species are not as prurient as humans when it comes to sex. Well, except for the Gargaxians, but that is quite understandable given all the spikes."

Richard smiled and began unbuttoning the shirt Wing had provided for him. "You sure know how to talk dirty, baby."

Wing walked up and put her arms around him. Even in space, Richard felt at home with the heat of a female body pressed up against him, flesh touching against flesh. Wing's body was lithe and utilitarian, clean of all body hair or fat, two parts but small breasts mounted on her chest and staring proudly out. Her bare sex was puffy and already a bit moist as she pressed it against his legs. "Sarcasm is the lowest form of humor, you know."

And then she pushed him back and was on top of him on the bed, kissing him. Wing's lips pried his open and her tongue slipped tentatively inside. She had a virgin's curiosity, but none of the accompanying shame and uncertainty. It was a curious mix between experience and innocence, and one that made Richard hard as a steel bar as he taught her to French properly.

He felt his pants melting away, rejoining Wing's mass of matter. Only his boxers, his last real possession, remained. The wing was grinding herself up and down on his hardness, staining his underwear with a combination of their eager juices.

Richard reached up and grabbed a hold of one of her breasts, rolling the nipple roughly between his fingers. Wing gasped. "That feels good," she said. "Do it again." And so he did.

He found that Wing's human body was soft and responsive, pliant beneath his caresses. When he reached down to her sex and ran his fingers along her moist slit she practically jumped. Richard was beginning to feel the familiar joy of taking a woman, of making her dependent on his touch and attention until he felt merciful enough to send her to the moon with a monster orgasm.

Richard sat up, rolling Wing over onto her back. He stripped off his boxers and left them at the foot of his bed. He loomed in front of her, his erect cock like a twitching one-eyed monster, but her expression held no fear. Nor did it hold much at all, but he tried not to focus like that. Wing's legs parted like butter and he positioned himself between them, rubbing the head of his cock up against the entrance of her slick warm sex.

"You sure about this?" he said. "You know, for human women, the first time can be pretty painful."

"You don't think I'd be silly enough to give myself a virgin body, would you?" said Wing.

Abductor or not, Richard was beginning to like this alien. Of course, this was the very definition of Stockholm Syndrome, but he wasn't about to pass it up. He pressed forward, nudging the head of his cock between her tight lips, and then slowly pushing the rest of his manhood inside her.

Wing let out a long breath as if the penetration was forcing the air out of her. Richard rested a moment in her steamy wetness. It felt just like the real thing. Maybe a little better.

He began to thrust, slowly at first, but quickly picking up tempo, the way he always did with inexperienced girls. Her pussy was tight like a vise, and Richard had to concentrate to stop himself from spurting in her prematurely. Wing started gasping as if surprised at the jolts of pleasure going through her body. Richard was pressing down on her, their skins touching everywhere, wet bodies grinding up against one another.

Still, the blank expression on Wing's face was starting to get to Richard. He pulled out, eliciting a murmur of disappointment from her. "Get on your hands and knees," he said, and Wing obeyed. He leaned in to lick her sopping pussy and Wing squealed with delight. He didn't finish eating her out, but just gave her a taste of the wonders of good tonguing before pulling back and getting up on his knees to fuck her from behind.

"So Wing," he said, easing his cock into her. "You can look like anything, right."

"That is correct," said Wing's human body, panting.

"I've never gone for the butch type. Let's do long brown hair... tits a bit bigger... pale skin, mid- 20s. Can you do it?"

Richard half expected to get slapped, but Wing simply complied. Her hair changed color and slithered out of her scalp, her skin blanched before him, and her breasts inflated like balloons. The changes in her body created strange shimmers around his cock. Richard thought he might have found his dream girl.

With a savage thrust, Richard started fucking Wing in earnest. She responded to his increasingly frantic speed with faster gasps and moans and even began to thrust back. Richard had one hand on her hips and used the other to maul her now larger breasts as he let his primal instincts take over. She felt so good, so soft and hot and eager beneath him. He was beginning to lose himself.

Richard slung a leg over Wing's hips, practically standing up behind her, and started fucking her with shorter, shallower strokes. She mewled like all of the girls he had in the past, all of the one-night stands and short-lived girlfriends. Within moments her breathing was labored and she was burying her face in the pillow, surrendering to him completely.

Wing's orgasm was a literal earthquake. The vessel around them shook and rattled as she screamed out her climax into the bed's pillows. Assorted pieces of furniture vanished momentarily. Richard just held onto her hot body and enjoyed the vibrations traveling through her cunt, clinging to the only stable thing in the world.

He decided to give her a moment to recover, although his hard cock was still embedded in her. Richard clung to her backside, the sweat sticking their skin together. "So what do you think of the human orgasm?" he whispered into her ear.

"Better than most," she said. "Not as good as the Lira or the Cnaut but hey, whose is?"

"Remind me to get with one of those," said Richard with a chuckle. He resumed slowly thrusting in and out of her, taking his time to savor the delightful squeeze of her flesh. Wing looked back at him, a grin on his face, and that was when it hit him.

She was Kayleigh. The hair, the skin, everything... he had asked her, in not so many words, to change her shape into that of his graduate student. The impression was inexact, but it was the same body as he had felt bucking against him that night in the conference, astraddle him and covered with a sheen of sweat, muttering sweet obscenities...

He needed to get her out of her mind. It was just a meaningless fling, the kind he'd had so many of. But she had replaced all his other fantasies. When he jacked himself to orgasm, it was always that night he thought of. He even thought of her when he was with other women -- including, apparently, Wing.

Richard knew he needed to stop this. "Can you do Scarlett Johannsen?"

"Pardon?"

"You know, the movie star? Can you look like her?"

Wing chuckled. "Ah, the celebrity thing. Sorry, but I haven't had much time to study your popular culture in depth."

"Forget it. Just do blonde, big tits, double Ds, no waist but a big ass. The vapidest slut you can manage." Richard was half surprised at the rage he found welling up inside him, but it didn't turn him off. The anger -- anger against himself and the situation and Wing and women -- fused with the arousal pulsing through his cock to form powerful, insistent sexuality, sexuality made to hurt people.

Wing's body was shifting under him, growing into a caricature of a porn star. Her hair bleached, the color vanishing into the ether. Richard mauled her big floppy tits, leaving scratch marks across them, and she gasped at the sting of his nails. He grabbed her by her blonde tresses and shoved her face down into the pillow.

He heard her muffled cry, not sure whether of pleasure or alarm, but at this point, he was beyond caring. Richard hammered into Wing as fast as he could, wanting to punish her cunt, wanting to own and ruin her and turn her into a mere flesh-hole, a sheath for his dick and nothing else. He wanted to pour all his anger into her, make her feel the pain and confusion she had caused. It was raw, mean, animalistic sex and it felt fucking great.

Richard clutched her waist tightly, nails digging into her soft skin, as he felt his orgasm approach. The sound of his hips pounding against her ass was deafening. Finally, with a long angry cry, he shot his seed inside her. It felt like he was coming for a long time, sending rope after rope into her hot womb. The orgasm wasn't so much the pinnacle of pleasure as it was released in its purest form. Suddenly sedate and unemotional, Richard rolled over onto his back, breathing heavily.

The wing was just staring at him, her face as blank as ever. Her pale skin was still marked red from where he had grabbed and scratched her. Richard could see his pearly cum dripping out from between her puffy red nether lips.

"I'm sorry," he said after a while. "I got a bit carried away there and--"

"It was okay," said Wing. Richard realized he had no idea how she felt -- these surface pleasantries were all he would get. "After all, that's part of human sex too."

Richard couldn't help but laugh. "You do it once, and suddenly you're an expert on human sex?"

Wing dipped her fingers down between her legs, and brought them up to sample Richard's cum. She shuddered with distaste. "I'm an outside observer -- well, I was fifteen minutes ago. I can take a more objective perspective. You're a scientist -- you must know that an outsider can see things that the people directly involved can't."

She had a point, but one that made Richard want to slug her. "Well, if you didn't mind it..."

"I recognize that you're angry with me, and as I said, you have a right to be. No way wouldn't play out in our coupling. I would advise you not to worry about it." And with that, she was melting into the bed again, and then Wing's freshly-fucked human body was gone.

"Not one for cuddling and pillow talk, eh?" said Richard. Well, he wasn't either. And there was nothing worse than talking with someone who thought they understood you but didn't.

It was near a week into the journey, and Tom and Kayleigh had shared a bed every night ("night" being, once again, something of an abstract concept), but they hadn't had sex, hadn't even made out. On the second night, Tom had put a hand on her thigh, his usual subdued invitation, and she had shuddered and mentioned for the hundredth time how weirded out she was about some alien constantly watching, feeling them. He hadn't tried anything since then.

On the sixth night, he confessed. "You know, I hate to say it, but this is kind of exciting."

Kayleigh rolled around to face him, her look accusatory. "How can you say that? We're never going to see any of our friends or family again."

"I know, I know," he said. "But I mean, think about it. When I was a kid, I thought my whole boring life was just a prelude -- that one day I was going to trip over a portal or a magic ring or a radioactive animal or something and I would be in a fantasy or sci-fi story, because that's what I read and that's how I thought life went. But time went on, and I had to learn that probably wasn't going to happen. And I was depressed because I couldn't stand the thought of being normal and boring forever. And now I feel like... maybe, as a kid, I was right after all. I just needed to wait longer."

Kayleigh usually smiled and gushed about how cute his flights of fantasy were, but she wasn't in the mood. "Great. You just go on thinking about how you're in a big sci-fi fantasy, and try to ignore the fact that we're being violently kidnapped."

"Well, the two things aren't mutually exclusive, you know." Kayleigh rolled over and ignored him.

What Tom felt like saying was that he had gone through this already, when he followed Kayleigh across the country for her school. He had already said goodbye to his friends and family and made peace with seeing them only on holidays. He had decided that Kayleigh was better than everyone else put together and that he would follow her to the ends of the Earth. If it turned out he had to go even further than that, so be it.

The ship shook suddenly, and they found themselves clinging to each other, hearts beating rapidly in fear. The quake ceased quickly, but they didn't break off for a while. They sat and listened to the vague sounds of flesh slapping together and male and female moans of pleasure.

"What the hell is going on in there?" said Tom.

Kayleigh rolled over and buried her face in the pillow. "I don't even want to know."

Tom thought that maybe Richard had convinced Wing to summon him up to the porno movie or something. He had to be lonely, isolated from the couple that was spending all their time together. It was weird how even in this strange situation the same old social dynamics -- the third wheel, for instance -- still held power.

He got up and went to the window, set to display the genuine landscape. It was completely foreign -- almost a parody of the night sky he knew. Stars were in the wrong place or nonexistent, and strangely colored planets glowed dimly in the distance as they passed by. It was -he had to admit -- intoxicating. He couldn't help it. Whatever lay ahead, he was excited to get there.

But the journey continued a quiet stroll through a seemingly endless night.

Chapter: 3

It was like a long, intermittent dream. There was no sense of time on the ship, and little to do. Richard was rarely awake for more than a few hours at a time, and he spent those hours in a daze, wandering out to fill himself with the bland food Wing produced, sit, and think about the strange circumstances he was in, then return to the warm comfort of his bed. He rarely saw Tom and Kayleigh -- maybe they were on a different sleep cycle, maybe they just never left their room.

He thought frequently about conjuring up Wing and her (his? Their? Not for the first time Richard lamented the inadequacies of the English language and its gender pronouns) transformable body. But he didn't want to dredge up any more of the weird shit lingering deep in the recesses of his mind. Sometimes he would feel a caress through the sheets as if the ship was propositioning him, but he would always turn over and dig his head further into his pillow.

Many days passed like this -- he wasn't sure how many. Time was meaningless here. The strange, slippery dreams he had were hard to tell apart from his reality. And then, for the first time in a while, Wing summoned them all to the living room.

Tom and Kayleigh were dressed in matching bathrobes, which they pulled around them as an almost instinctive gesture of self-protection. Richard wondered if they had gotten Wing to conjure up an entire wardrobe for them. He then realized that he hadn't showered or changed clothes the entire trip, which might explain the distance the couple was taking from him. He thought he smelled fine.

Today Wing had once again formed his authoritative male human appendage. "Hello once again," he said. "I hope your journey has been pleasant thus far."

Kayleigh sniffled. "About as pleasant as kidnappings get."

"Please, I believe the appropriate term is abduction," said Wing.

There was a pause. "Wait, was that a joke from you?" said Richard. "I'm shocked."

"Humour is another one of the base pleasures I occasionally indulge in," said Wing. "But I haven't called you here for my comedy routine. First off, I'm pleased to tell you that we are three of your Earth days away from Jian-2. We've made good time if I do say so myself. But before we can land you will have to be inspected."

Richard sighed. "I knew there was going to be anal probing somewhere."

"You know, this fascination with anal probes that your species has, and projects onto others, is quite fascinating," said Wing. "I wonder what kind of subconscious desires are responsible for this fantasy?"

Kayleigh didn't laugh -- she hadn't smiled in at least a week. "So tell us what you're going to do to us now."

"A representative of the New Species department will run some tests on you with highly advanced machinery. He won't even have to touch your physical bodies."

For some reason, Richard wasn't reassured. Still, there was nothing he or the other two could do to resist -- even if they did somehow escape the eternally malleable prison that was Wing, there was nothing outside but the deadly vacuum of space. It was just as Kayleigh had put it -- it wasn't a question of what they would do but what Wing and his alien cohorts would do to them.

And yet, Richard couldn't bring himself to hate Wing in the same way Kayleigh did. Rationally, she (as Richard thought of the being if only to reassure himself about his sexuality) was their kidnapper and jailer, the villain of the story. But Richard didn't regret being torn away from a life of endless department meetings and fruitless experiments. Maybe it was just Stockholm syndrome or residual endorphins, but he liked Wing -- at least as much as one could like a creature that was so vastly different.

But he saw the dead stare in Kayleigh's eyes and almost forgot about all of that.

The three abductees gathered around the viewscreen for the first thing they had been able to see out of it that wasn't stars set in a velvet void. This spaceship looked much different than the sleek, almost familiar chrome vessel they were currently sitting in. It was a gnarled brown hunk making its way through space on a pulse of purple flame. The ship was lumpy and amorphous, far from an example of aerodynamic engineering.

They sat in silence, watching it grow from a small discolored dot on the horizon to something massive making a slow but inevitable lurch towards them. Tom thought that the exterior shell of the alien ship looked like wood, but surely that was impossible. Wing swung itself to the side, allowing the other ship to dock alongside it, and formed a connecting tunnel out of thin air. With a swish, a door opened in the floor, and then suddenly the floor was a wall and they were all drifting softly downwards as Wing rearranged itself (when it was just a ship, it was hard to not use the pronoun "it") to accommodate its new visitors.

The creatures that emerged from the door might have resembled humans, were it not for the lack of heads. All four of their limbs ended in six-fingered hands. They crawled around the room on all fours, grasping and swinging from one piece of furniture to the next. Two were male and one female, although the only sign of sex was the genitals visible behind the back set of arms. Every inch of their tangerine-orange skin was exposed. Three gashes on their backs pulsed, taking in and releasing air.

Tom stepped back, repulsed by the creatures. They seemed like grotesque rearrangements of human beings, some sort of mad science experiment. He wanted to run, but there was nowhere to run.

This wasn't what he had imagined space would be like.

Richard and Kayleigh both looked queasy as well, although there was more than a hint of fascination in their eyes. If the aliens recognized the humans' anxiety, they didn't show it, strolling around the room confidently (at least Tom thought it was confidence, although it was hard to read emotions into something that didn't have a face.)

"These are Thalians," said Wing, back in his authoritative male human form. "This is part of their Science Corps they've donated for League's purposes. There's no reason for alarm -- they're here on official business."

Tom couldn't help but stare at one of the Thalians' cock, drawn in close to its body. Other than the orange coloration, it looked strangely identical to the human instrument. Now that he was closer, he could see four small holes on the front end of the creatures' torsos -- perhaps some kind of senses.

A pungent, foreign smell hit the air. It smelled a bit like paprika, but even that was a bit of a stretch -- Tom couldn't truly relate it to anything he had ever smelled before. He supposed this would be a common experience, encountering the completely new -- something that was not just a modification of something he already knew but built on a foundation he was completely oblivious to. It was exciting and terrifying. He felt like a child.

Kayleigh was squatting down next to one of the creatures, examining closely the pulsing gashes in its back. (His back? Her? These things had genitals, but did they have genders?) She had her scientific look on, that gaze of scrutiny and fascination that Tom recognized from the few times he had seen her in the lab, or the many times he had seen her curled up with some scientific journal.

"How do they communicate?" she said.

"Through scent," said Wing. "In fact, at this moment they are greeting you, quite respectfully I might add."

Kayleigh put her hand out, as though she was going to pet the alien, but withdrew it at the last second. Tom heaved a sigh of relief. He saw one Thalian crawling closer to him, and instinctively shied away.

"Now they are asking for you to come over to their ship for the tests. I believe they don't want me listening in on them." If Wing had been more familiar with human gestures, he might have raised an eyebrow.

"Onto there?" said Richard, gesturing towards the strange Thalian ship with a mixture of disbelief and panic. It was understandable -- the Thalians seemed like much more of a threat than Wing did, strange creatures they couldn't understand. The wing was the type of movie villain who seduced you with luxury and killed you with kindness -- which was a threat in and of itself, but all things considered, Tom supposed he would much rather be killed by kindness than by weird headless aliens.

"No need to worry," said a new voice. "You aren't in any danger." Standing in the doorway was the first other human any of them had seen in weeks.

He had dusky bronze skin and his words had a strange accent -- perhaps he was from a different country on Earth, or perhaps he had dragged a rusted English language out of mothballs. Whichever it was, Tom was sure it wasn't another illusion, another being disguising itself as human-like Wing did. He was too imperfect, too flabby and earthy, completely unlike the movie stars Wing unwittingly conjured up as its avatars.

The man was wearing loose-fitting black clothing that wouldn't have looked out of place on Earth. He stepped forward and offered the three abductees his hand. Tom and Richard shook it hesitantly, while Kayleigh just stared at the preferred appendage like it was obscene.

"Xanon Por Pramuk," he said. "Special Envoy for the League of Worlds. When I heard that we had some humans heading our way, I had to tag along with the usual science ship."

"So you're with the aliens, huh?" said Richard. "Sort of a human Uncle Tom, I guess."

He continued smiling blithely. "I'm afraid I don't understand the reference. I'm seventh-generation diaspora, you see."

Tom was trying to put the implications together in his head. "Meaning..."

"My ancestors got whisked up from Thailand about two centuries ago. I was born on Talos-9. I am afraid I have not kept up much with Earth culture -- we get so little of it, just fragments here and there. People tend not to be abducted with libraries."

Tom had thought that they would be the only humans where they were going. He was comforted by the knowledge but there were more, but now felt just ignorant -- had alien abductions been happening for centuries? How long had this been going on? Just how many abductees, and descendants of abductees, were there up there?

"But you will find out about all this in time," said Xanon. "You will be living amongst the human population -- Little Earth, for lack of a better term -- on Jian-2. All we need to do are a few preliminary medical and psychological evaluations."

Tom backed up. It sounded like code for something sinister. Xanon chuckled. Wing's human embodiment said "I'm aware that you may be paranoid, with good reason. But they truly are harmless tests. We wouldn't bring you all this way to harm you."

Kayleigh shivered again, one of those full-body shudders she had been doing lately like she was trying to contract herself into a small cube. "Paranoid? It's not paranoia. You kidnapped us. Don't act like we're silly and irrational to resent that."

Wing said nothing, just gestured towards the door. Tom still didn't want to go, but he didn't think he had any choice. He stepped over the barrier into the strange wooden Thalian ship. Richard and Kayleigh stepped in after him. Were they following him? Had he been appointed the leader without realizing it?

Xanon cleared his throat. "I am afraid we're going to have to leave all of you behind, Wing."

Wing smiled, although it was an awkward approximation of a human smile. "Of course. I had forgotten." Tom felt the incredibly disconcerting feeling of his clothes sliding off his body, going from solid material to a crawling liquid that pooled on the floor. He had almost forgotten that their clothes were a part of Wing, and that shock overtook any shame at his sudden nudity. He looked at the black pool slithering across the threshold back into Wing's ship body, where it melted into the ground. He wondered if that liquid was the closest thing Wing had to a true body.

Xanon showed no reaction to their nudity, and they were too battered to protest. Even Kayleigh didn't make much of an effort -- she crossed her arms to cover her breasts but left her pussy standing uninhibited in the artificial air.

"Come on in," said Xanon. "We may be able to get you some real clothes."

As soon as they were five feet away from Wing they found themselves floating off the ground. Kayleigh grabbed a nearby branch and pushed herself off it, sending her floating slowly through the air. Tom tried to grab for a perch and ended up spinning himself into an opposite wall. He didn't need a science degree to figure out that there was no artificial gravity on this ship, but that didn't help him navigate the confusing tumble that the world has become. As soon as he had decided on one point being a wall and another being the floor he would spin and all that would be reversed. Xanon was watching with a profound sense of amusement, hanging on to one looping branch.

"A little help?' said Tom.

"Just grab onto the sides and climb. You can propel yourself for a while if you do it right -- treat it like swimming. She has a good form over there." Indeed, Kayleigh was breast-stroking her way through the gravityless air. Tom had to catch his breath. She looked like an angel, flying nude through the sky. She also looked, just maybe, like she was enjoying herself for the first time since they had left Earth.

The strange plant-like skin of the ship proved a boon for traveling in zero gravity, perhaps why it was there. The rough wall was covered in roots and vines, which were convenient handholds as Tom slowly climbed along. He had to go into more of a squatting position as he climbed, wary of rubbing his twig and berries against the ship's rough bark. This meant sticking his butt out into the air, causing Kayleigh to snicker as she looked past. Richard was blessed with boxer shorts, so he hugged tight to the wall. Out of the corner of his eye, Tom saw the Thalians easily scurrying across the walls, their four hands always finding purchase somewhere. He had the sneaking suspicion that he looked like a complete idiot.

Tom realized he should have been marveling more at the ship. It was his first glance at a real ship, instead of the malleable floating hotel room. But his mind was mostly taken up by the difficulties of putting one foot in front of the other, and the remaining mental power went towards worrying about what the tests would involve.

Up ahead, Xanon tossed them each down a robe, although his throws were weak and the robes floated through the sky like great bats. Tom managed to tug it on, although it did send him spiraling into the opposite wall. At first, he thought the robe would be too big, but it quickly shrunk and constricted to fit the contours of his body. It wasn't much, he thought, but at least it was a real piece of clothing.

All along the plant corridor were torso-sized silver circles, the metal awkwardly juxtaposing with the natural environment around them. Tom wondered how a ship like this even worked, how it stayed sealed against the vacuum of space. Xanon reached one of the silver circles, seemingly the same as all the others, and tapped it twice. It whisked open, revealing a smaller room behind it. Xanon invited them all through, although it took a couple of tries for Tom to get through the portal without bumping his head up around it.

The room they moved into was similar but smaller, a wooden sphere with more silver portals on either side of it. A seamless black sphere floated in mid-air. Xanon propelled himself over to it. "All right, who wants to go first?"

The three abductees looked around at each other, each looking queasy. Xanon dug a finger into the black ball and pulled it back, splitting the material open and forming a makeshift seam. He took a green cylindrical instrument out of it, with several odd-shaped buttons on it.

Tom sighed. He didn't want to have to go through this, whatever it was, but he would make sure it was okay for Kayleigh. Besides this, something was exciting about even a sketchy medical examination -- the zero-gravity, the new technology, the strange aliens. It was every bit as novel as it was disconcerting. "I'll do it."

Xanon ushered Richard and Kayleigh out of the room. The silver door slid shut again. Tom kicked his feet awkwardly, propelling him back towards the opposite wall. He would have to watch his movements here -- even the slightest habit was exaggerated into ridiculous motion. Xanon approached with the green sensor. Tom was feeling a lot less confident now that he was alone with this stranger, a human who might as well have been alien.

"Do I need to undress?" said Tom.

Xanon shook his head. He pressed a button on the sensor and started running it over Tom's body slowly, starting at the feet. It cast a pale blue light against Tom's skin, and the areas it touched seemed to crawl, although he was sure he was imagining that. In a way, it was just like the doctor's office, without the smell of disinfectant.

"So," said Xanon. "How are you dealing with leaving Earth?"

"Okay."

He raised an eyebrow. "Okay? I am going to need more from you than okay."

In all the worry over the green sensor, Tom had forgotten that Xanon had even mentioned a psych examination. "I'm doing fine. I miss home and shit, but I'm kind of excited to be here and see new things. I feel like this is still kind of a dream... like maybe it hasn't sunk in for me. Hell, maybe this is a dream. It'd be a very strong dream, but that's more reasonable than me being in space right now."

"It is not a dream," said Xanon. "Denying what is happening shall not do you any good."

"I'm not denying it. It's just like... I know what's happening, but it's like I'm following the plot of a movie, not what's happening in my life." Tom wasn't sure why he was opening up to Xanon, but it felt right.

"What about the other two?"

Tom felt especially unsure about dishing out Kayleigh and Richard's struggles. "Well, you're going to see them after me, right?"

Xanon paused and tapped his hip. Tom had no idea what it meant -- maybe it was an alien gesture that he had picked up. "Well, I would rather get every perspective I can."

"Well, it's hard to say about Richard -- he keeps to himself a lot. Maybe he's bawling his eyes out in there, maybe he's fine. As for Kayleigh... I'll admit it, she's taking it rough. Rougher than I would have expected. But she'll bounce back. She's a strong girl."

Xanon made a non-comittal "mm-hmm" noise. The green scanner had reached Tom's neckline. "How have Wings of Steel treated you?"

"Well, he -- is, I guess -- has been fine. A bit reluctant to explain things, but it's provided us with everything we need. Truth be told, I forget it's there sometimes... and then when I do remember, it's kind of creepy, you know? Or maybe you don't."

The scanner continued its advance, up towards his face. "Close your eyes, please." Tom complied. A second later he could see the bright green light of the strange device through the dark red shield of his eyelids. He felt a headache quickly blossoming.

A moment later, however, the light ceased. Tom felt a finger trying to open his mouth, and he complied in a daze. The finger -- Xanon's, he presumed -- slipped a small, smooth capsule onto his tongue and retreated. "Swallow it," said Xanon.

"Can I open my eyes now?" In the process of speaking, Tom swallowed the pill, whether he wanted to or not he was still unsure).

"Go ahead." Xanon had in his hand a bottle of pills that looked to be the same size as the one he had just administered. It looked weirdly similar to an Earth prescription pill bottle. "It's just a simple adaptation medicine. The atmosphere of Jian-2 is only a bit different than Earth's, but that bit will cause quite some damage if you don't take these. Once daily, before you go to bed. Don't forget."

Maybe Tom's initial impression of a doctor's visit wasn't too far off. "Is that it? Are we done now?"

Xanon looked at a stream of characters running along the side of the green device. "I think so. You are healthy physically and mentally doing about as well as could be expected. Half of the people I see have gone completely insane by this point."

"That's encouraging," said Tom. He wondered if Xanon grasped sarcasm, or if that was a distinctly Earth-ian concept.

The space-born human just offered an officious smile. "Great. Can you send in the next person?"

Tom floated out towards the steel circle he had entered through. Hesitantly, he tapped it, and it let him pass. It looked fancy, but he wondered whether a simple door would have been better.

Three of the creepy Thalians were standing around looking at the humans -- well, maybe they were looking. They didn't have anything Tom could immediately identify as eyes, and their brains were a complete mystery to him. "It's nothing to worry about," Tom said to his companions. "Just a check-up. Who wants to go next?"

Richard and Kayleigh looked at each other, disbelieving. Richard stuck out his fist and they silently rock-paper-scissored for it. Kayleigh's paper was quickly cut in twain by Richard's scissors.

"I guess I'll get it over with." Kayleigh hauled herself through the portal. Tom tried not to look up at her robe as she kicked it away perpendicular to him.

"I'm going to go back to the ship," said Tom. "I mean, our ship. Wing. This is giving me the creeps. On top of the inhuman Thalians, he still didn't grasp how the plant-like ship -- a living, pulsing organism beneath him -- managed to work, and was worried that in another minute or so the rest of the universe might also realize how silly it was.

It took him a little while to get back to Wing, as he tended to crash into walls or spin in the wrong direction. When he landed facefirst in Wing's common room, he let out a sigh of relief so heavy it surprised even himself. He had never thought that this ship would feel like a sanctuary, but at least it had gravity and square rooms and looked like a goddamn spaceship should.

Kayleigh kicked off the edge of the sliding circle portal to reach the center of the spherical room, remembering a childhood full of swig and gymnastics lessons, and grabbed onto Xanon's arms to stop herself in the middle. She felt the novelty of zero gravity, but only as a small twinkling light through a heavy barrier of clouds For the past week she had felt as though the edges of her vision were fraying, or that a dark frame was closing in on her. Everything else felt far away and vaguely distorted like she was underwater. She slept a lot, partly because that was the only thing to do onboard Wing, and partly because it was the only time she felt good.

Xanon put his hands on her shoulders to steady her. "Are you good now?"

Kayleigh wasn't sure, but she knew she wasn't flying out towards the wall again. "Yeah." Xanon let go and the two of them stood there, floating still in space.

He was scanning her with his medical devices, but she couldn't take her eyes off him, his body. Perhaps it was just the novelty of the first new human she had seen in a week, but she thought there was also something subtly strange about his body -- it was longer, lighter, and slightly different proportions than the men she was used to seeing. And that dusky skin, the lightly rippling muscles underneath his clothes...

A question. He had asked her a question.

"Sorry, can you repeat that?"

"No problem. How are you dealing with leaving Earth?"

Leaving Earth, as if it had been a voluntary process. "How do you think? I want to go back."

"But you know that is impossible."

For the past week, or however long that eternity had been marked on the calendar, Kayleigh had a monologue running through her about the injustice being done to her, the sorrow she was feeling, and how everyone she had known may as well be dead. But now she felt as though she couldn't say all that. Instead, she just insisted. "You don't understand. I need to go back. So many people depend on me."

Xanon looked up from the display of his device. "Listen. I get a lot of people -- humans and otherwise -- coming through here, and they are all upset and worried. But you know what? They always end up all right. Everything is going to be all right."

"How can you know?"

"Have a little faith in us," said Xanon softly. "To be honest, I do not agree with you being taken. But we will do everything we can -- me and the other people in the league -- to help you go on."

Kayleigh threw herself into the arms of Xanon, the medical instrument being knocked away. Xanon put his arms around her and breathed her fragrance deep. She didn't know why she had been overcome with emotion, but she was. It was a simple act of comfort, but an unexpected one, and perhaps that made all the difference.

"Hold on," said Xanon. "Be careful around here, you might break something."

Kayleigh reached up to run her fingers through his hair. His light muscles pumped lithely against her thinly-robed body. He was lean and perfect, man bared down to his sexy essentials. She felt a growing erection pressing against her robe. "Do you want to fuck?" The words came out of her without passing through her brain first, but it seemed like the only thing that could be said here.

"I am sorry," Xanon said. "My English vocabulary isn't the best. What does 'fuck' mean?"

She wondered whether he was being genuine, or just playing around. In any case, it didn't turn her off. "Well, I guess I'll have to show you." Grabbing Xanon by the neck she pulled his lips down to her, slipping her tongue into his mouth almost immediately. He reciprocated, running his tongue along her gums and reaching up to grab her by the ass. Kayleigh thought that guys were pretty much the same anywhere in the galaxy.

Xanon broke off from the deep kiss. "So that was fucking?"

"Oh no," said Kayleigh. She quickly undid the belt on her robe and shrugged out of her lone piece of clothing. The robe floated away, down towards the ground, and she was there in her nude, pneumatic glory. Xanon's eyes drank her body in with a more than medical interest.

His hands were soon all over her, running up her thighs, kneading her ass, spinning her around, and roughly grabbing her breasts. Kayleigh pressed her body up against him, feeling his clothed hardness nestled between her plump ass cheeks. His touch sent little electric shocks wherever it went, and even innocuous motion drew out gasps from her. With every jolt of pleasure the darkness that had been surrounding her mind for the past week seemed to dissipate, as though Xanon's touch was a wind blowing away the fog enshrouding her. This was what she needed, she realized: sex, communion with another human body, to bring her back to the present instead of the lost past or the uncertain future.

But it was with the wrong guy. She should have been doing this with Tom, or even Richard, instead of some guy she had just met. But with him, it was so easy, her pussy got wet on its own. She felt almost as though there was a force apart from her, moving her beyond her inhibitions and, and making her love every minute of it.

She needed him inside her, to make her forget about all this crap. Kayleigh frantically tried to peel off Xanon's clothes, but no matter how normal they had appeared, they had ties and buttons in strange and unfamiliar places. She accidentally slipped away from him while tugging hard on a mysterious strap, but he quickly caught her.

"Be careful," Xanon said. "You have to hold on tight."

"You sound like you've done this before."

Xanon only raised an eyebrow in response. He covered her neck in kisses, leaving a hot trail across her clavicle. Kayleigh could feel him shifting down there, but she couldn't quite see what he was doing, and the soft warmth of his lips made her not care.

Then his black outfit came undone in one movement, snapping away from him and into a black ball that drifted to the other side of the room. His lightly muscled body was lithe and his naked legs seemed to stretch on forever from her perspective. A half-erect cock, uncut, hung between those long legs. His body was completely hairless. He was human and alien at the same time, a combination Kayleigh found strangely intriguing.

She drew herself down his nude body, wanting to feel this new, youthful hunk against her. It was perhaps that sensation of newness she craved, that of being surprised in the most delightful ways. She dragged her weightless breasts across his washboard chest, feeling the softness of his skin intensely through her inflamed nipples. She kept going down, but instead of having to kneel or crouch, there was just more down. It was as though they were two bodies alone in the universe, able to extend themselves infinitely in whatever directions they pleased.

Kayleigh nestled her head in his pelvis, inhaling that intoxicating masculine scent. His cock was rising, hungering for her breath, dreaming of her lips. She looked down at it, so close, and knew she had to have it.

Xanon let out a long grunt as she took the heavy head of his cock into her lips. Some things didn't change across the galaxy -- men still regarded a good blowjob as one of life's miracles. Kayleigh kept her hands on Xanon's hips so as not to fall away, and slowly ran her head down his shaft and then up it again. She grazed his cock skin with her lips and occasionally with just a bit of tooth, the way Tom always liked it. When she had reached the end of his head again she let go of the cock with a satisfying pock and took a big lick along the underside of his dick as though it were an ice-cream cone.

And then it was the same thing again, but a bit faster and a bit harder, drawing out another impassioned moan from Xanon. Kayleigh liked that he wasn't silent in bed like so many men she had dated -- maybe that was exclusively an Earth thing. She picked up the tempo until she was constantly bobbing up and down on his cock, loving the feeling of his warm girth filling his mouth.

Then he was spinning, and her world was spinning, and she no longer knew what was up. Xanon grabbed her thighs to steady her, and it was only then that she realized that he had spun around into a 69 position, all while keeping his dick in her mouth. Kayleigh liked a man who had some agility in bed -- or out of bed, as the case was now.

With the first flicker of his tongue on her pussy, her stream of thought was annihilated by a burst of pleasure. His touch was gentle but skilled, managing to evoke stabs of pleasure with the lightest of touches. And when he slid one finger into her by now sopping wet snatch... well, it was simple perfection. As he rubbed her inner walls all sorrow and pain seemed to be a million light-years away, belonging to a completely different person.

Somewhere Kayleigh knew that if she didn't keep sucking, keep reciprocating, all this might end. So she sucked Xanon's cock for dear life. And as she left a trail of wet, sloppy spittle over him, his tongue delved between her lower lips and sent her to new heights.

Kayleigh began to feel that tension building in her, that tightness in her chest that always precipitated a monster climax. It was as if the pleasure pulsing through her cunt had decided to gather there, instead of flowing out to the rest of her body, but now was about to explode to the very edges of her skin.

Then he was suddenly gone from her pussy and out of her mouth, and he was spinning around again. Kayleigh had to duck his legs to keep from getting kicked in the face but managed a grin by the time his handsome face -- complete with the shine from her juices -- came up again. "You ready?" She could feel his slick hardness at her entrance.

The last remnant of a doubt threw itself onto the battlements of her mind. "Do you..."

"I have an infertility chip." He chuckled. "Strange. I forgot that you would have to worry about something like that. In any case, do you want to... what was the expression... frag me?"

"Good enough," said Kayleigh. She grabbed hold of his warm shaft and guided it inside of her. Xanon relaxed and let her take control. With a hand on his ass, she pressed him deeper inside of him, until she reached her limit. That warm, hard flesh filled her She felt complete.

Xanon wrapped his arms around her, caressing her shoulder blades. Kayleigh kept a tight hold on his ass, kneading the cheeks in the same way she liked hers to be caressed. They floated there for what felt like an eternity, enjoying the overwhelming feeling of warm flesh against warm flesh, and the fullness of their connection. Then they started rocking. It was hard to say who started the movement, but both threw themselves into it and what was at first a slow, gentle thrusting quickly grew faster and harder.

There was no top or bottom here, just two bodies entwined and thrusting against each other as if trying to merge. The fuck had its rhythm, bigger than either of them. The lack of gravity empowered Kayleigh -- not only did the thrusts travel through her body without any kind of impediment or absorber, but their mid-air position also made her feel so far away from the dark outside world and everything in it. There was nothing else around her but this man and his body, and that suited her perfectly.

She stopped being able to tell the difference between his thrusts into her and her manic humping against him -- it was all one rhythm, one event. They held on tightly to each other, sweaty skin smashed together, incoherently whispering their astonishment into each others' ears.

Instead of falling to the ground or forming a wet spot on the mattress, their sweat and juices stuck to them, forming a thin cocoon of sex around them. Perhaps at a different time, Kayleigh would have found this disgusting, but it just seemed to give greater meaning to the act--she was bathing in Xanon, bathing in herself, but most of all in this strange but wonderful thing they were able to do together.

The rhythm was fast and fierce now, and Kayleigh felt that tense build-up of pleasure in her cunt once again. This time she wouldn't be denied. She ground herself up against Xanon, scraping her nipples against his hard chest, taking his stiff cock as far in as she could. "I'm close," she whispered.

"So am I," he said.

And after that brief moment of connection, they were racing for the finish line, thrusting against each other furiously, each in desperate pursuit of their own pleasure. Kayleigh came first, and it was a monstrous orgasm that absolutely tore through her. She forgot that she was suspended in mid-air, forgot about her infidelity or what infidelity even meant, forgot everything except that she was a gooey mass of ecstatic pleasure.

Xanon finished soon after her, shuddering as he shot his spunk inside her. Kayleigh realized that her throat was sore. Had she screamed as she came? She couldn't remember.

He pulled out of her with an exhausted gasp. Their combined juices flowed out in a stream and then stopped, forming a strange physical arc as if to commemorate what they had just done.

The revulsion hit Kayleigh in one massive wave. All of a sudden the outside world came crashing into her mind, and the implications of her random carnal act -- another betrayal of Tom, another betrayal of herself -- struck her mind. And then there were all the old thoughts, about the injustice and the futility of her situation. She wanted to curl up into a ball and beg them to leave her alone for another few minutes, at least let her enjoy the afterglow, but they were already upon her.

She pushed away from Xanon, letting herself float to the edge of the room. She didn't want to be near him. He was a sign of her mistake, her absolute sluttishness -- but maybe that was too kind. Whorishness. She was a whore.

Xanon looked puzzled. "Are you okay? I was not too rough, was I?"

Kayleigh shook her head, an action that made her hair floating in a strange hazel curve. "It's just... we shouldn't have done this."

"Why not?" said Xanon. "I enjoyed it."

Kayleigh wondered if this was alien morality, that there was nothing wrong with banging someone you had just met. If so, she didn't want any part of it. "Never mind. We should clean up. I don't want the others to know what we were doing."

"If you say so. I think I have some wipes somewhere around here."

True enough, in the bottom of his strange spherical container Xanon had a pack of wet wipes, which they both used to sponge off the film of sweat that clung to them. It took a while, chasing down the spare bits of their juices that had flown off and now floated freely around the spherical room, and then careening around as she struggled to put her clothes back on. She caught Xanon chuckling at the last bit, and shot him a dirty look.

"Well," said Xanon. "While I would love for you to stay and talk, I imagine your friend must be getting fairly impatient."

"What about the check-up?" said Kayleigh.

"You seem plenty healthy to me." Xanon chuckled. "Vivacious, even. I will give you my doctoral stamp of approval. Just remember to take these pills daily, and you should stay fit."

Kayleigh didn't feel healthy at all.

After half an hour, most of which was spent trying to ignore the shrieks and grunts coming from within, Richard's number finally came up. Even if he hadn't heard anything, the freshly-fucked look on her face told the story. And this was accounting for the natural dishevelment brought on by zero gravity. But given the circumstances, she seemed strangely unhappy. 'You're next," she said, before propelling herself back to the safety of Wing.

Richard knew he shouldn't be disturbed by that. After all, if she was willing to cheat with him, she would be willing to cheat with others. Still, he had thought that he was something special, that there was genuine affection beyond the usual grad student/supervisor mutual exploitation. And now he had found out that he was just a convenient hard cock.

He suddenly realized that he badly wanted to get away from Tom and Kayleigh, who over the past two weeks had come to seem more and more like moping, irresponsible children. He wanted to deal with his equals, or better yet his superiors. Well, he guessed that he would have to deal with this check-up before he could escape into this brand new world full of interesting people, or maybe not-quite people.

Xanon had a breezy, devil-may-care attitude that he hadn't sported before. He began to scan Richard up and down with his device, a process that made the professor profoundly uncomfortable. "So how are you holding up?"

"Okay," said Richard. "Better than most would, I think. I'm trying to keep all this in perspective."

"And what perspective is that?"

"That a few years down the world, I'll probably be grateful. That's what keeps me going on those nights where all I want is TV and some fried chicken."

Xanon nodded his mind far away. "And what about your fellow travelers? How are they handling the shock?"

"Well, you've seen how well Kayleigh is doing," said Richard, a sardonic note creeping into her voice. "And Tom? Tom's okay. Seems a little out of it, but I didn't know him beforehand. Maybe that's normal for him."

"She is a remarkable girl," said Xanon wistfully.

"She certainly is," said Richard. But he wasn't sure whether he believed it anymore. On Earth, she had always seemed a font of boundless energy and creativity, soaking up knowledge faster than anyone Richard had ever met. Hell, she might even fit under the nebulous definition of "genius" -- she had certainly come up with a few things that even Richard hadn't thought of before, taking new approaches that suddenly seemed blindingly obvious. And her giddy energy in bed...

"Close your eyes." Richard dutifully obeyed and could see even through his eyelids the light of the scanner. He felt a headache coming on. Then there was a hand groping his face, which he promptly slapped away.

"What, you want to fuck all of us?"

Xanon looked somehow offended and amused at the same time. "Please, Richard. I was only trying to give you a pill." He pointed to a capsule now floating in the air.

"Well, you don't have to be so hands-on about everything." Richard reached out and gulped the capsule down grudgingly.

Xanon put his hands behind his head as if reclining in mid-air. "So, how have Wings of Steel treated you?"

"Like pets, honestly," said Richard. "Providing, but condescendingly. Although if she's a pet owner, there's a bit of bestiality there."

"Oh? Do tell." Xanon's interest sounded more than professional.

"Do you think I'm some kind of gossipmonger?" said Richard. "Oh, let me rephrase that: do you want me to be some kind of gossipmonger?"

Xanon seemed to completely miss the implicit threat of revealing his tryst with Kayleigh, or perhaps he didn't care. "Well, I do always like a good story."

"Wing and I had sex once. Well, I had sex with a human-shaped part of her."

"What was it like?" Xanon had the breathy glee of a voyeur in his voice. "You know, I have always fantasized about being with an Erusmi. It must be the ultimate experience. Everything you have ever desired, no matter how strange or depraved... well, assuming the Erusmi is open-minded."

Richard slugged Xanon across the jaw. He just had too many reasons to.

The diasporic human spun with the force of the impact, slowly drifting until he hit the wall of the sphere. He kept a shit-eating grin on his face the whole time.

"Are we done here?" Richard said.

"You can go," said Xanon. "Or you can stay if you want." He bunched his fists and licked his lips, a chimeric provocation.

Richard let himself out, tapping on the portal the same way he had watched Xanon do it. His first encounter with the galaxy at large had not exactly been the brave scientific exchange he was hoping for. He was starting to feel distinctly disquieted about the whole situation.

The Thalian ship pulled away with a lurch, shaking Wing and the three humans inside it. It drifted off for a while before shooting off into the darkness of space with a burst of purple flame. Richard had gotten a notebook and pen from Wing and was frantically trying to sketch out the ship, both its exterior and interior. In the margins, he scribbled wild speculations as to how it could work.

"You know, I could explain how that ship functions if you want," said Wing, its feminine voice bouncing out from nowhere.

"Save it," said Richard. "I want to try to figure it out myself. If I can't get the answer, then you can spoil me."

Before they had left, Xanon had given each of them League ID cards. When tapped a tiny holographic projection of them in their new black robes emerged from the card's green surface. The image was perfect and could have been mistaken for the genuine article if it wasn't two inches tall and deathly still. There was no other text on the card, but Xanon had said that everything was in a computer chip.

"You know, this is kind of creeping me out," said Kayleigh. "I mean, is this a totalitarian state or something? Why do we need ID cards? And a physical examination, with weird pills..."

"The League of Worlds is a free association for mutual benefit--"

"Can the propaganda," Richard said, cutting off Wing's spiel.

Tom was playing with his card, tilting his tiny miniature around at different angles and dangling it upside down. "I dunno. I mean, we need ID to do a bunch of stuff back on Earth, and Xanon said we can use this to get free food and housing. To be honest, it sounds a lot better than what we came from."

"Oh, then that just makes this all perfectly okay, doesn't it?" said Kayleigh.

"I didn't say that."

Kayleigh looked as though she was going to break down again, but instead, she breathed in deeply and exhaled patiently. She looked up with a forced smile on her face. "You're right, you didn't. I shouldn't take this all out on you."

"We can't judge anything from what we've heard so far," said Richard. "When we get off this ship, we need to keep our eyes and ears open and judge for ourselves what kind of world we're living in." It was, perhaps, the default response of a scientist, but Richard thought it was the best option right now.

Wing appeared next to them in female form, the shape she took when she wanted to be comforting. "That sounds like the best approach. I've tried to be as unbiased as possible in what I tell you, but even I'm not perfect."

Kayleigh chuckled. "You don't say? Well, I'll be in my room. Let me know the next time we have to go out."

"I'll come with," said Tom, as though they were going out to the mall and not just pacing between the limited space available to them. They vanished into their bedroom.

Wing stood there, looking like a wax statue. Presumably, she had no idea how creepy this was. Or perhaps she did and was just in the mood to intimidate Richard.

"Remember to breathe," said Richard. "It's probably not necessary for you, but humans look strange if they aren't doing it."

"Oh yes, of course," said Wing. Her chest instantly began to rise and fall, perfectly in time with Richard's own. "My apologies. It's very easy to forget these things -- the small details, you understand."

Richard couldn't help but smile wryly. "Right." It was interesting to see these little chinks in the armor of Wing, an imperfection in a being that so frequently seemed to be a god. "I was wondering... could you make this ship bigger? It's getting a little claustrophobic. Or is there a limit to how much matter you can produce?"

"My power is not unlimited," said Wing. "I can stretch my boundaries, but it takes some effort and is unstable. This is close to how much I can do reliably. I could make your living space bigger, but as a consequence, it would be much more Spartan."

Richard imagined a giant concrete cube hurling through space. "Got it. What about sex? Does that take energy out of you?"

It was still a shock to him when she didn't blush. "It doesn't take much energy at all. As I said, I can get as distracted as I want and keep this stable."

"Really. Shall we test your concentration?" Richard leaned in and nuzzled her neck, drawing a surprised cry from her.

"Like I said, concentration isn't really an issue... but if you're propositioning me..." Wing had at least managed to affect a smile this time, albeit a fake-looking one. Her inability to cotton onto proper human displays of emotion was getting to be kind of endearing, especially in how it contrasted with her seeming omnipotence.

"I think I am propositioning you." Richard what had gotten into him. Maybe it was Xanon's boasts and crude questioning. In any case, he wanted Wing and the blank canvas her body promised.

She kissed him hotly. Whatever kind of eleventh-dimensional sexual desire Wing possessed was now inflamed. Her clothes vanished into her body, leaving her in that perfect nudity -- those pert but large breasts with their bubblegum-pink nipples that seemed to defy gravity, that round plush ass, the thin body that extended to unreasonable curves in just the right places, and the gorgeous, sweetly innocent face to tie it all together. She was the kind of girl you only saw in pictures, a model made into a superhuman beauty through the aid of hours of makeup, manipulate lighting, and careful Photoshopping... but without all of that, in the natural flesh. Maybe Wing thought that most human women looked like this. It was certainly the impression she would get from TV or movies.

She was kissing his neck and tugging at his robe. Richard checked back nervously behind him. "We should get back to my room. You know, before Tom or Kayleigh comes out to mope."

"You know," said Wing. "It's always a disappointment to find out your cute new species has a sex taboo."

"Sorry for my irrationality," said Richard, backing up towards his room as he did so.

"Don't apologize," she said. "That irrationality is what makes you interesting." And then she was somehow ahead of him. He followed the hypnotic sway of that perfect ass into his bedroom.

Richard didn't even wait until the door was sealed behind him before tackling Wing to the bed. She giggled and bucked against his weight, but was apparently content to be pinned there. He slid down her back until he reached those two glorious globes and promptly buried his face in them.

"Mmmmm," said Wing, burying her face into the pillow. As Richard began licking the little pink entrance between those big ass cheeks, she let out a contented sigh like she was at a spa. Richard just slid further into her behind, licking up the preternaturally clean valley. He wasn't normally much of an ass man, but with an ass like this, who wouldn't be?

His cock was hard as a steel bar and all of a sudden he needed to be inside her, now. Today was not a day for foreplay -- in fact, right now he didn't care very much about Wing's pleasure at all. Why should he? She could surely conjure up an orgasm for herself out of thin air.

Grabbing her thigh he turned her over and positioned himself at her entrance. Without waiting for a response from her he rammed into her cunt. Wing winced. "I wasn't ready yet."

"Get ready. Lube yourself up." It was dry down there, and while the aggravating friction suited him at the moment, the last thing Richard needed was a chafed dick.

"What?"

He waved his hand. "You can conjure up all this stuff, you can conjure up some pussy juice. Just hurry up."

"Seduction on Earth must be very primitive indeed," said Wing. She closed her eyes and Richard felt a quick flood of her juices over his cock. It just kept coming, as though from a faucet and was soon pouring out of her full pussy and onto the bed.

"Okay, that's enough."

"Just making sure."

Richard began thrusting way in earnest. He grabbed two handfuls of her tits and used them as a handhold as he rode her furiously, bucking against her with every ounce of force he could muster. He left big red marks on those bounteous breasts, even a couple of scratches from where his nails had dug in. Experimentally, he slapped one of them and then did it harder. Wing kept crying out in some mixture of pleasure, pain, and surprise -- but, of course, her face remained as blank as ever.

He ignored that and slammed into her again and again. By now he was drawing almost fully out of there and then thrusting into her until their hips smashed together like thunder. He slid easily into her now, and he suspected that not all of the lubrication was artificial. But he didn't care. All Richard cared about right now was that feeling of raw, blissful achievement -- conquest.

All of a sudden this wasn't enough. Xanon's words rang in his ears. Why stick to missionary with a blonde bimbo when he had an entire sexual fantasyland at his fingertips, softly responding to his touch?

He paused, filling Wing up to the hilt. "Can you be black? Er, I mean, like an African-American girl."

"Well, I've never been to Africa or America, so that might be an issue," said Wing. "But I know what you mean." Her skin seemed as if it was going through the world's most intense tanning process. From a soft peach color, it ripened into a hard brown, which then darkened into ebon black flesh. Within a moment, Richard was fucking his first black girl.

For some reason, it seemed like more than a new paint job. Maybe it was that delicious contrast of Wing's dark skin with her cute pink pussy -- a pink that now seemed so much more bright and innocent. Or maybe it was the strangeness of those dusty brown nipples, or the general strangeness of this unfamiliar, exotic body. But Richard was suddenly consumed with desire and started thrusting into Wing faster and harder than ever.

"My word!" Wing grabbed onto the headboard of his bed for dear life as he rammed into her.

Her dark tits bounced back and forth with every thrust, or at least they did when Richard wasn't grabbing onto them roughly. She thrust back in turn, and the raggedness of her breath showed that this reaming wasn't entirely unwelcome.

Richard was panting and felt sweat running down his chest. His mind felt like it was on fire. Wing's pussy was just so perfect, and it was driving him insane. He had to fuck her, had to fuck her in every way possible. "Now do Asian."

Dutifully her skin changed again, this time blanching to a pale white, and her features drawn into a Chinese expression. Her frame was still the same, which looked slightly unnatural, but also like a too-good-to-be-true fantasy. And that just fuelled Richard even more. As he rammed into her again and again he realized that he could write his every adolescent desire on Wing. It would be foolish to pass that opportunity up. Of course, that was just the rationalization -- the driving force was this strange burning desire to ravish this woman, to ram his sex through her like an invading army and pour every ounce of his frustration into her.

Richard grabbed hold of one of Wing's legs and threw it over his shoulders, increasing his leverage as he thrust in and out of her. "Bigger tits," he barked. The part handful that Wing had already possessed grew into bodacious DD-cups. And they looked -- indeed, they were -- every bit as natural as the original set had been. He grabbed the soft pillowy breasts and kept a tight grip on them as he rode Wing. They still slipped away from him, their fat slick with his sweat.

"Bigger." They grew to freak-show proportions, drooping downwards. They felt heavy as he lifted them to play with. He licked one of Wing's enormous nipples and she shuddered spastically. Even with Wing's limited range of expressions, he could still see her shock at the sudden orgasm. "Bigger!"

"I'm pushing biology as it is," she said between pants. All this while Richard was keeping up his savage rhythm, slamming in and out of her. His cock had almost become numb to the sensation of her tight cunt clenching around him.

"I want to push biology. Make them as big as basketballs."

Wing looked skeptical, but her breasts swelled further until they were bigger than her head. Richard didn't even have to lean down to take one of her nipples in his mouth and suck, once again drawing full-body shivers, which coursed through her and made her pussy vibrate around him. "Oh fuck," he muttered. Wing looked like a teenage boy's wet dream beneath him, her face barely visible from behind her breasts. Richard felt vaguely delirious.

"Can you grow a second pair?" He lightly slapped her stomach, as if showing her where to put them. "Just as big as these ones."

Wing grunted, and there they were, burgeoning up and blossoming before her eyes. He stared at the four giant breasts, bobbing up and down with the force of his thrusts, slapping into each other and bouncing in every direction. Richard found himself salivating, dribbling a trail of drool across one of the massive mammaries.

He leaned in, closer and closer, slowing down his penetration. He pushed forward, trying to squeeze himself in the valley between her two sets of breasts. He wanted to know what it felt like to be surrounded by tit-flesh on every side.

And then suddenly he was falling, as though Wing's cleavage had eaten him whole. Around him, everything was red and wet and warm. Richard realized that he was within a fleshy membrane that pressed hungrily to every square inch of his body -- and that included his erect cock, which was rapidly being milked by the wettest and tightest thing it had ever felt.

Helpless, he came. He felt the cum shooting out of his cock in forceful arcs, and the pleasure that was like a battering ram to his torso. Richard's cock contracted for a moment and then started coming again. Stars shot in front of his eyes, and then he was blind. His body was just some exploding edifice attached to his cock, which was still pumping and shuddering

Richard spurted once more into the void, and then everything went dark.

When he came to, his body felt exhausted from pleasure. It was like he had overloaded his nerves and burnt them out. He couldn't move his legs, but it didn't seem like a big issue.

The wing was standing alongside the bed, back in her regular, two-breasted form, and clad in her respectable black suit. Richard weakly beckoned for her with his fingers. He had come close to this feeling after attempting a triathlon once, but this was still different.

"What was that?" he said.

"It was what you wanted," said Wing. "Something to fuck. Excess. So I gave it to you the best I knew how."

"Was that.... some kind of alien that you turned into? That I was in?"

"I was a form of my own devising. There are no species specifically created for human man's pleasure, no matter how much you may act otherwise."

Something was buzzing in Richard's head, and he couldn't quite figure out what. "Are you mad at me?"

"No, just a little... disappointed." There was an almost parental quality to Wing's sigh. She was learning quickly. "If you'll excuse me, I need to navigate us through an asteroid belt."

Richard felt as though his arm was made of the leg, but he still managed to weakly pat the pillow next to him. "Stay here. Cuddle."

But Wing was already vanishing into the walls again -- or, more precisely, vanishing into herself. "We're two days out from Jian-2. I recommend you think about some things. The world out there will not be so... accommodating."

Richard couldn't think about the future right then, especially not the eternity of two days away. All of his exhausted mind's power was going towards his attempt to untangle the paradoxical feeling running through him. How could he feel so good and so bad at the same time?

Chapter: 4

Jian-2 was a planet a lot like Earth, except with the continents and the oceans scrambled and rearranged. To Richard, it looked a bit too much like Earth. It took something away from his home planet to imagine that it was not all that uncommon, that they could find similar planets all across the galaxy. Quite frankly, he had been hoping for something more exciting.

They all stood by Wing's "window", an artificial but (hopefully, at least) truthful representation of what the world outside looked like. Wing coasted silently towards the planet. Tom stood in awe of the sight, and even Kayleigh looked a little impressed through her detachment. What Richard noticed was all the things that weren't there. There were no jumps in gravity, no change in motion as they entered Jian-2's orbit, and most importantly the lack of anything artificial-looking in the planet's atmosphere.

"No satellites," he said out loud. Nobody responded.

Wing entered the atmosphere like it was nothing but another chunk of space. They were immersed in greyness, but there was none of the rockings and panicked rumbling that Richard had been expecting. It was almost like some quaint 19th-century fantasist's idea of what a journey to another planet would be like.

And then they were out of the atmosphere and into the clouds, white cotton-balls that seemed to spiral out vertically as Wing sliced through them at the same calm gait. Richard forgot his scientific mind and joined the other two in standing agog at the window The continent was growing beneath them, unfurling itself to reveal mountains and valleys and tiny twinkling cities that were growing at a tremendous pace. As they approached closer Richard could see that there were six cities, all seemingly of equal size, standing in a kind of ring in the continent's most fertile spot. From their distance, what seemed to be a circle of light connected all six. And then they were diving in even closer, and in a split second the city beneath them was the human size, and they were looking out on a seemingly endless plain of skyscrapers poking out from an unseen ground like spikes on a hedgehog's back.

Richard tried to catch his breath. Kayleigh turned to him and grinned. "Don't go in much for urban sprawl, do they?"

Wing's voice, back to being male and authoritative, decided to chime in. "We make the most efficient use of our land possible, to leave the most space for agriculture and natural environments."

Kayleigh raised her hands in surrender. "Yes, yes, you've developed a utopia. We get it."

"Once you've lived in our society, I will take your judgments of it entirely seriously," said Wing without a hint of sarcasm. "Now, if you'll just stick close together for a moment, I'm going to shrink a bit so we can fit on your roof."

Kayleigh linked arms with Tom. Richard edged closer to her, feeling weirdly guilty for following instructions.

Wing drew in suddenly and all at once. Their rooms and all the space they had been accustomed to were folded up into their ship's steely walls quicker than the eye could process, and for a moment Richard was afraid that they might all be crushed. But Wing stopped short of their bodies and instead left them in a stark bedroom-shaped shit. He then glided softly down to land on one of the grey tower roofs.

"I'd say wait until the plane comes to a complete stop," said Richard. "But I think we're at a complete stop already."

"How can you tell jokes right now?" said Tom. "And especially bad ones?"

"We all have our own ways of working off nerves."

And then Wing did something Richard had half convinced himself it would never do. It let them out.

The air smelt different. It was strange that that was the first thing he'd notice, but it was. It was purer, like deep country air, but also there was a strange tinge to its scent that he couldn't quite place. The second thing that struck Richard was quiet.

There was a faint rumbling far beneath them, but other than that it sounded like they were alone in the skyscraper city. He began to get the impression of this as a hermeneutic, sealed-off world, with the buildings just massive mausoleums beneath them.

"Where is everybody?" said Kayleigh.

They had only had their backs turned for a second, but during that time Wing had become his officious human male persona. "You must remember, we are very high up. People mostly stay inside, but there is a street environment down below, as humans prefer." Those two words -"street environment" -- sounded strange and sterile on Wing's newly-fashioned tongue. "Of course, one can receive all amenities without ever stepping foot outside."

"Why would you set up a world like that?" said Kayleigh, Her tone wasn't angry -- more wistful, with a little curiosity in there.

"Mainly out of convenience," said Wing. "But honestly, I don't understand this obsession humans have with the setting."

Richard had nothing to say to that -- here, in this bizarre array of silver stretching out to the horizon, the setting seemed like the most important thing imaginable.

"Now," said Wing. "Please stand on this center tile and I will show you to your quarters.

Wing indicated a metallic four-by-four spot on the roof, only faintly visible. The abductees crowded in uneasily. They were forced into proximity, squeezing against each other, although this was not too great an imposition on their privacy. After all,

Richard figured, he had fucked two of the three others -- what was wrong with a little group hug?

"Down," Wing gravely intoned. And then the floor dropped out from under them.

Richard realized quickly that this was it: this was when he was going to die. They were plummeting down a dark shaft, wind whipping past them, floor falling just a bit quicker than they were so that they seemed to be perpetually hovering above it. He clung to Kayleigh's hand and prayed that it was swift and not especially painful. And then, they stopped, a little startled but no worse for wear.

"Richard?" said Tom. "Was that you screaming?"

"You were all screaming," said Wing. "No need to be afraid -- the technology is perfectly safe. Welcome to Floor 343 -- Madrid, as its inhabitants have dubbed it." A doorway had opened on the left side of the chasm, letting a bright light in to reveal the area as a roofless but nevertheless pretty standard elevator.

What was distinctly not standard was the area around it. They were under an impossible sunny blue sky. Whether the light was natural or artificial, it shone down on a quaint cobblestone square, a kind of old-world nostalgia piece. The steps all lead up into identical villas, which stood on a circular perimeter, all facing inwards. The exception to this was a ground-level bakery which glowed warmly from the inside. The only thing stopping this from being a little self-contained universe was two sets of spiral staircases, one on each side of the elevator, which stretched up into the sky and down into the earth below. It looked decidedly bigger on the inside than it had on the outside. Of course, it was hard to consider this "inside" at all.

Tom gazed up at the ceiling sky with faint amazement. Kayleigh was silent as well, but it was more of a suspicious quiet as she dissected the indoor block with her eyes.

"Not bad," said Richard, hoping he sounded nonchalant. "Does it go dark at night?"

"Of course," said Wing. "Our goal is to make the transition as painless as possible."

"The past couple of weeks hasn't really been painless," said Kayleigh.

Wing's facial expression was his usual mask of blandness, but beneath it, Richard somehow detected that he was perhaps a bit tired of apologizing. "Your... helper should be here shortly. In fact, I believe she is running late."

"Helper?"

"The precise term I am thinking of stems from the Veranti language -- it means something akin to 'person who allows you to live. I am not aware of any English equivalent."

Richard rolled the phrase over in his mind. "Person who allows you to live" was probably meant to sound kind and parental, but it also sounded a bit like a kidnapper, or some warlord extending mercy to his fallen foe.

In the windows of the weird little villas, he could see faces peeking out, cautious but curious. There were a couple of children and a couple of things that were not human. Before Richard could look much closer at it he was distracted by the sound of metallic footsteps echoing up from below.

A human blur burst out from the stairs on the ground. Richard saw a flash of short black hair as what was eventually recognized as a petite woman ran up to them. "Sorry sorry sorry! I am having the worst day -- my alarm didn't go off, and there was a jam in the tunnels, and then my key card didn't work until I reconfigured it and you just have no idea how sorry I am..."

Now that she was only talking a mile a minute and not moving that fast Richard noticed some distinctly strange things about the newcomer. For one thing, her right eye was red while her left one was blue, something that would have seemed pretty mundane if not for the small blue text he saw in the red eye. She was human, but her movements seemed strange, almost too smooth and too fluid. Oh, and her right arm was carved out of glistening chrome.

Everyone was a little stunned by the girl's appearance as well as her personality. Tom was the first to compose himself. "It's okay. We just got here too. And, uh, by 'here' I mean the planet. God, that feels weird to say."

"You'll get used to it," said the girl. "Of course, I wouldn't know, really -- I'm third-generation. Oh! I haven't introduced myself. Stupid, stupid. My name's Mona. M-O-N-A. But you could probably figure that out. I don't think you guys are dumb or anything. God, what's Earth-like these days?"

"It's doing pretty good," said Tom. "Well, it might all flood in a couple of decades, but right now things are cool."

"Cool! Anyways, I'm the ambassador of this floor -- people call me the Mayor of Madrid. It's, like, a joke. I'm not really in charge, I just like volunteering for stuff. Like welcoming you here!" Mona's babble just seemed to get faster and faster, until it took a conscious act of translation to understand her.

Richard finally spoke. "Why Madrid, if I could ask?"

"Most of the cool city names were taken. Like, Rome is floor 3 here, from way back in the early days. But Madrid's cool too! Running of the bulls and all that. That's Madrid, right? I know it's Spain. Somebody already took Barcelona, which is weird because I would have thought that Madrid would go first. Maybe that's where they run the bulls. Barcelona, I mean. It sucks for the new floors that have to pick really obscure cities. Or some lots go with something completely different for a name, but the abstract ones ran out way quicker anyway. You guys are lucky we had a few vacancies. There was a couple that left to go make a quad over in another tower, and Steven joined the Diplomatic Force and got assigned to Battas-12, which is pretty unlucky, but like I said, good for you."

Richard was still trying to process all of that, and maybe add to his very hazy understanding of this alien world, when Tom, possibly having already given up on all of that, spoke. "Can you show us around?"

"Oh! Yes. Of course. That's what I'm here for. Listen to me babbling."

It wasn't much of a guided tour. Their new homes were all quaint small houses with mostly conventional furnishings other than a couple of strange metallic appliances that Mona, in her mile-a-minute monologue, never thought to define. Tom and Kayleigh had inherited the homes of the couple, who had built a connecting passageway. The bakery looked like it had been transplanted directly from the 1950s, and operated more as an anachronism than anything else. Kayleigh regarded Mona with an ever-increasing look of bile.

"It's a very nice-looking cage," she muttered under her breath once. Tom and Mona were too far up ahead to hear it.

Richard picked up the pace until he caught up with the more cheerful pair. "So. Are we going to get jobs? Money?"

"You'll be provided for," said Mona. "But most people here apply for assignment of some form or another. It gets you some extra spending credits. But I wouldn't worry about that. Just try to adjust for now. Here, you want a donut?"

Richard frowned. He had never been the kind of guy who could sit around doing nothing for very long. For him, working -- contributing to some larger project -- was adjusting. But he said nothing and ate the donut, which looked and tasted a bit strange, but was still delectable. He wondered if any of these advanced alien races had cracked the secret of making junk food that was good for you. Probably not.

Mona had continued blathering about something or other after Richard had long tuned her out. She looked up at Richard with her seemingly permanent perky smile. "So, any questions?"

"Too many," he said. But he didn't think he was going to get any answers.

The first thing Tom did when he and Kayleigh were left alone tried out the couch in his new place. He had spent entirely too much of his college years crashing on uncomfortable, scratchy friends' couches and as such was extremely pleased to discover that this one was soft as a dream. This was technological advancement, he supposed -- the little things being a little nicer.

Kayleigh was leaning up against one of the walls as if testing its stability. She looked grumpy, which was at least an upgrade from the generally empty stare she had had for most of the trip. Tom patted the seat next to him and she shuffled over to him.

"Don't tell me you like this place," she said.

"Well, it's not paradise, but it does seem very nicely run." He took her dangling hand in his. "Look, we'll figure out how to get back to Earth. Maybe we can be special ambassadors or whatever. But for now, we have each other, and that's enough."

"You sound like some cheesy rock singer."

"I think it was Bon Jovi. But he was a wise man."

"They. It was a band."

"Wasn't that also the main guy's name? Bon Jovi? His lawyer calls him Mr. Jovi?"

Kayleigh giggled. Tom kissed her hand, and then she was falling on top of him, giggling warmly into the side of his neck. Their bodies still fit together well. Kayleigh straddled him, kissing his ear.

A knock at the door interrupted whatever was going to happen. Kayleigh sprung up and dusted herself off. "I, uh, should probably get that."

At the door was a cheerful redhead who looked to be in her late 20s, carrying a fruit basket, as well as some sort of giant bird-man. Tom practically did a spit-take. The woman thrust the basket forward. "Hi! I'm Caroline. Your new neighbor. I saw you guys moving in and..."

"Thanks," said Kayleigh, taking the basket from Caroline without looking at it. Her eyes were fixed entirely on the bird-man. "And this is..."

The alien (because that was obviously what he was -- although really, so were all of the humans here) responded with a single word that seemed to go on and on. It was perhaps less of a word and more of a shifting sound or a song. "This is Esh Ku Tan Avana, but you can just call him Esh. He's a dendra." She said something to Esh in a similar sing-song moaning, presumably his language. "Oh, I should probably explain -- Dendra's vocal cords can't really deal with English words or really any human language. All that stopping and starting, you see. For what it's worth, I can only do a loose impression of their speech too. Esh has managed to stop laughing at it, but when his mother comes over..."

"I guess some things are universal," said Tom. He wasn't sure what the relationship was between these two, but it was closer than one would think from looking at them.

Caroline just blinked at that. "Yeah, and some things aren't. But don't worry. He can understand everything we're saying.

"Do you want to come in?" said Kayleigh, doing the best impression of a smile she had been able to do for a couple of weeks. Tom seemed to lose a big weight when he saw that smile, one that he hadn't even been aware he had been carrying around.

"Sure. I saw you moving in and, well, I just wanted to say hello... I know it can be very overwhelming at first." Caroline and Esh took a seat in the living room. Tom hoped Esh wouldn't leave feathers everywhere.

Now that he could get a closer look at the alien he saw that "bird-man" was a bit of a simplification. Esh stood seven feet tall and stooped to enter the house. Pillow-white feathers covered the backside of his wings and extended down his back and to the crown of his head, while his underbelly was decorated with scraggly yellow fur. He had generally humanoid features, save for the curved, sinister-looking beak. He balanced on three sets of arms, or perhaps talons, with hardscrabble black skin. He moved awkwardly on these limbs but made no motion to sit down.

"I'd normally get you a drink or a snack or something," said Kayleigh. "But I think the cupboard is bare." Esh shrugged a gesture that looked entirely inappropriate on him. The alien drew up his middle limb and rested the black hand/claw on Caroline's knee. It at least looked opposable. "So, um, do you two both live in this neighborhood? Floor? City?" It occurred to Tom that he would have to entirely change his routines of small talk.

"Well of course," said Caroline. "You see, Esh is my -- well, that's another thing in his language that I have trouble translating, but I would say 'lover' is the closest equivalent."

Tom blanched. His mind naturally leaped to the specifics of that arrangement, but even then he couldn't fathom it. He involuntarily glanced at the alien's crotch, hidden beneath a network of white and red sashes that served as clothes. Was that even possible? Biologically? Moreover, who would want to have sex with something that looked like that?

But he bit his tongue before he said anything. He didn't want to sound like a bigot -- or worse, some scandalized country boy just off the farm. He was sure this was normal around here. Hell, the whole galaxy was probably a vast intermingling of species much stranger than Esh, who at least resembled a strange combination of Earth animals. Was that what attracted Caroline to him?

In any case, Kayleigh seemed to be having as much deciding on an appropriate reaction.

Caroline looked back and forth between them, her eyes seeming to settle on the silence that was a palpable, physical presence there. "It's okay. I get a lot of that. Gape all you want." She displayed herself with an exaggerated flourish. It was a little self-congratulatory as if she had been trying to shock them.

"That's great for you," said Tom, deciding that the distinct feeling of grossed-outness he was going through was simply irrational. "Kayleigh and I are lovers as well." The word "lovers" was strange on his lips, old-fashioned and yet explicit at the same time. "Maybe we can have a double date sometimes."

Caroline smiled. "Cool. It's great that you guys got picked up together."

"How is that great?" said Kayleigh, her bitterness rising back up to the surface all at once.

Caroline held up her hands. "Well, I just mean that it's better than you being apart. I mean, if Tom here was abducted alone, you might never know what happened to him. You might think he ran off on you or he was dead or something."

Kayleigh cast Tom a look that said, in the least insulting way possible, that she might have preferred that alternative. And it had certainly crossed Tom's mind that his life would have been very different if he hadn't felt like doing something nice for his girl that particular night. But he was here, and his mind burned with curiosity not satisfied by the cryptic way everyone here around here seemed to talk. (Although perhaps what he saw as crypticness was just them taking the world around them as a given not worth discussing.)

"I guess so," said Kayleigh. "I'd rather we stayed on Earth, though."

Caroline shrugged. She had an almost sedated smile on her face. "Everything happens for a reason -- or at least that's what I like to think. I was pretty scared when it happened to me, but if it hadn't I would have never met Esh. So, things work out."

"And I'm sure there's some human man on Earth you would have liked to meet too," Kayleigh countered. "You can't just look at your life as it is and say that things had to happen a specific way to make it like this, and therefore destiny."

"I never said dest--"

Kayleigh was on a roll. "You said the boring, banal translation of it. Things happen because things happened in the past to make them happen. That doesn't mean that there was some divine hand making sure everything worked out all right for your love life. I mean, how would you even disprove that idea?"

Caroline just blinked repeatedly. "Um... you're probably right. Sorry, I didn't mean to..." She trailed off, evidently uncertain of her offense. Kayleigh had a steely look in her eyes, but Tom knew there was some happiness behind that. For a moment she had snapped back to her old self, or at least a fraction of it -- the rigid rationalist debate-clubber who good go on a thirty-minute rant about religion at the drop of the hat. It wasn't his favorite side of her, but it stemmed from that enthusiasm that she had seemed to lose during the trip.

Tom stepped in. "Okay guys, this isn't a debate. Let's just sit down and have a -- wait, what do you people drink around here."

"I have a case of AirSynth in the fridge," said Caroline. "Beloved by hundreds of species verse-wide. At least that's what the marketing says."

Esh squawked.

"Oh, come on. You love it too."

More of his strange, flowing language.

"You do not prefer LightningSynth. When I buy it, you never drink it." She turned back to Tom and Kayleigh. "Esh likes to pretend he's a lot more unconventional than he is. Anyway, let's head over to my place. You can fill me in on Earth news, and I'll show you how to work an XP station."

Some people were so determined to be your friend that there wasn't anything you could do about it. Still, even socializing with a pair of overly-peppy girls and a weird bird alien was, after two weeks on a tiny ship, a bit like that first lungful of air after almost drowning.

"So, what do you say this thing does again?"

Quinn adjusted the dials on the strange metal cylinder that looked to Richard like the world's most sophisticated trash can. "What does it do? It does everything. And yet it does nothing, not really."

"Enough with the koans, wise guy."

"The what?"

"Koans. They're a Zen thing. They're like riddles, except you solve them by realizing how or why they're unsolvable. Or something like that. I was never a fan."

Quinn sniffed the air and found it unpleasant. "There are so many weird Earth things that none of us know about. They bring us broadcasts from Earth, but it's always educational stuff -- presidential debates and science programs and such. And of course, that doesn't tell you a thing about the world itself."

"Well, what do you want?"

"Porn. You people have porn down there, don't you?"

Quinn was, Richard thought, the most alien human he had ever seen -- more than the cybernetic Mona, the effortlessly flying Xanon, or even the expressionless human form of Wing. His face was scrunched up like a rat's, and what's more, he huddled up like one, a single sweaty ball. He was middle-aged and not aging gracefully, and when he talked there was an aroma of tobacco mixed with something Richard couldn't recognize that came along with his speech. His skin was unusually gray, the only sign that there might be something non-human in his genetics. If that was even possible if across the galaxy the whims of fate had made another race close enough to humans to reproduce with them. (Said whims of fate had certainly produced creatures that humans could fuck, as Richard knew full well, so it might not be as outlandish as it seemed.) In truth, he didn't look that different from any of his home planet's skeevy guys smoking outside porno theatres. But Richard didn't want to admit that he and Quinn could belong to the same species.

As soon as he separated from the others, he made his way to his new bedroom and stripped out of the makeshift clothes Wing had fashioned out of itself. They had promptly started slithering away from him and out of the house, looking less like clothes and more like strange fast-moving giant slugs. Richard had tried and mostly succeeded at not being disturbed by that. Instead, he had sat down on his bed and reveled in being finally, even momentarily, alone.

And then, of course, there was the knock at the door, and he was scrambling to stuff himself into one of the (eerily precisely-sized) generic dark clothes that he had been provided with. And who should be at the door but a somewhat creepy-seeming neighbor who pressed his way into the house and declared that he must demonstrate how the XP station worked or else Richard's life would be hopelessly impoverished?

"Let me explain," said Quinn, after a bit more tinkering. "The XP immerses you in an imaginary world. Nothing you see or hear is real -- so, in that sense, it doesn't do anything. But in that world, anything that you want could happen, and it looks and feels just like the real thing. So it does everything. The XP is short for 'experience', and that's what it does -- it gives you an experience. If you catch my drift."

"You know," said Richard. "You could have just said 'virtual reality and saved us a lot of time."

"Virtual reality? Is that another one of your koans?"

Richard decided to ignore the terminology barrier and inspect the device a bit more. It had precious few external parts or displays, being mainly a smooth cylinder, with a couple of unmarked buttons and a slot on top. Quinn produced a nondescript grey card from his pocket and let the machine slurp it up. "There," he said. "That should get you some fun stuff."

"Um, what is that?"

"Let's call it an alternate set of programs. Most of the government VR offerings are tame -- you need to dig a bit for the good stuff." There was an air of skeeviness hanging over the whole thing, but Richard tried to withhold judgment. "Now, it looks like you're all ready."

"Do I need a headset or something?"

"Do you have a human brain?"

"I like to think so."

Quinn snickered. "Then you should be good. Just stay close to the machine and I'll rock your little savvy world."

"What did you just say? Savvy?"

Quinn looked more and more amused at Richard's ignorance. "Savvy. It means someone who's from a non-League world, someone that hasn't made it out into space yet. Stems from savage. No offense or anything."

Richard spread out his arms in a too-large gesture of acceptance. "How could I possibly take offense to that? Hey, what are you unscrewing there?"

A small rectangle of whatever chrome material the XP device was made out of came off in Quinn's hand. "Typical League design. They want to keep you from all the nasty stuff, but they're so accommodating that the whole machine just undresses for you and lets itself get hacked." Quinn fiddled around a bit behind the device. "There. Now it should be a bit more receptive to the good stuff."

"So what next?" said Richard.

"Next? We enjoy." Quinn slithered his tongue across the top pair of his lips. He hit a small white button, and instantaneously the world around Richard fell away.

He was floating in a blue abyss, soaked in low-level comfort. It was how he had felt as an undergrad stretched out with a book on the quad lawns, amazed at the warmth of early spring. Or those late nights at the pub in grad school, arguing string theory with his friends. It was the kind of happiness you were only aware of when it was about to end, and you got up with heavy legs.

Quinn was next to him, and he suddenly seemed much less repulsive. In fact, it seemed cruel to have judged him so harshly, to begin with. He was just a neighbor, trying to help a new arrival. Richard waved lightly to Quinn. "You were right. This is great."

Quinn snickered. "This? This is the lobby."

"Oh." Richard frowned. He felt like a yokel visiting the big city for the first time, neck craning up to see where the buildings met the sky. "Well, how do we get to the main event."

"First off, we shift over to our pirate module." Quinn had a pedagogically smug look on his face. He muttered a word that Richard couldn't make sense of, some strange amalgamation of overlapping consonants. The world around them shifted to an offensive, bright-red void. Richard was still strangely happy, but now it was happiness tinged with a bit of anger and a bit of fear. Maybe a bit like running an experiment, he thought.

Quinn smacked his lips. "Load XBrothel."

There was no fading, no gradual descent. Before Richard's mind could process it, they were in a cozy room with low lighting, sitting on an old-fashioned couch with only one arm. The whole room was covered in exotic-looking rugs and tapestries. The only exit he could see was thrown a silk curtain, although shadows hung in the corners and obscured much of the room. Sitting across from them, on a similar couch, was a mature-looking woman dressed in an elegant black gown. She had a gray streak in her hair and a knowing smile that made her in equal measure frightening and desirable.

"Um... hello," said Richard. He hated being amazed. "I'm Richard."

The woman's knowing grin grew deeper. "You can call me Madame... shall we say, Lucille? I've always liked the sound of that."

"Hi, Lucille. Uh, where are we?"

Quinn elbowed him in the side. "No need to be chatty. She's a program."

Lucille expounded with a faint Eastern European flair, like the last in a line of debauched aristocrats. "This is my house of iniquity. We can fulfill any desire you have, and introduce you to ones you never knew. Any fetish, any species, anything you want. If you just want to murder someone, we can accommodate you. We can do the reverse. But even if your interests don't run towards the exotic, we can offer you depths of pleasure you've never known before."

It was a rousing speech, and Richard found himself entranced by the cadence of Lucille's syllables. Quinn leaned in and whispered in his ear. "This is an old program, but this guy I know updated it and refitted it for humans. Not that we have to stick to humans..."

"So," said Madame Lucille. "What do you want?"

"What I want," said Quinn with obvious relish. "Is for you to suck my dick."

Even knowing that this was a world of virtual wish-fulfillment, Richard expected Quinn to get slapped and the two of them to be thrown out onto the streets of some virtual slum. But Madame Lucille simply got up, hiking her skirt as she walked around the table, and in as classy and as ladylike a manner as possible, descended to her knees and fished Quinn's dick out of his pants.

Quinn's cock had the same grayish tone as the rest of his skin, but the length was what got to Richard. It was like a piece of oversized sausage, and it wasn't even hard yet. Lucille burrowed herself into his crotch, kissing his heavy balls and rubbing the length of his cock against her cheek. She turned to Richard and said, in a sultry voice, "And for you?"

"I, uh... a girl. I want a girl."

"Coming right up." There was a momentary instability in the room, and a girl did indeed pop into existence. Specifically, it was a nervous-looking preteen girl, dressed in bright clothes that would have been adorable in any other context.

Richard rapidly stood up, shifting away from the girl. "Not like that! I mean, not a girl.

That's just wrong."

Quinn leaned back and groaned as Madame Lucille took his cockhead into her mouth. "Hey man, it's all virtual. Nobody gets hurt. If that's what you want..."

Richard was still in a panic, one that Quinn seemed to find most amusing. "It is not what I want.

I want a woman. An adult human woman. Like, in her 20s or something."

Lucille mumbled something affirmative around Quinn's cock. When Richard turned around, the girl seemed to have grown into a woman, and a quite fetching one at that. She also was wearing substantially fewer clothes. The blonde bombshell was contained in only a silky white set of tiny undergarments from which her milky flesh sprung joyfully. She appeared to have just walked out of a pin-up calendar.

Richard's throat was dry, so he didn't speak. The blonde walked over towards him. Her gait was like one of those optical illusions -- at one moment it was a controlled, seductive saunter, and at another, it was a hesitant, innocent but still drawn by some strange power of attraction. She stopped a few feet from him, her coral pink lips upturned with just the hint of a smile. He did the only thing that seemed natural and kissed her.

It was like kissing an electric fence. He pulled away from her abruptly, afraid of burning up in sensation. The blonde virtual girl just stood staring as he slowly tried to piece apart the raw roar of feeling still echoing within him. The kiss had been, upon consideration, the perfect kiss -- soft and hot and needful without being needy, that mixture of innocence and whorish desire -- no, not a mixture, both things existing simultaneously and twisted together into a delicious double helix. And it was the perfect kiss, but each aspect of that kiss has magnified a hundredfold. Her lips were as soft as wet clay, as hot as the sun, as innocent as the Virgin Mary, and as wanton as the Whore of Babylon. It sent an erotic burst through him greater than his strongest orgasm. His cock was hard as a steel bar within his pants.

"What... how..."

He turned to Quinn, who now had a dark-skinned human girl slurping on his balls, fighting for space alongside Madame Lucille. His head was thrown back in full-throated moans of pleasure, the dual fellatio apparently rendering him almost invertebrate. He turned one half-lidded eye to

Richard and his expression of shock. "Like I said, man. It's better than life. Otherwise, there wouldn't be much point."

Richard turned to the digital ingenue again. At first, the kiss had felt like too much, but as its sensations slowly faded they left a void within him. He wanted to feel that again. Or maybe he needed it. The line between the two seemed very thin.

So he kissed the blonde again, and it was just as good as the first one, but he held on a little longer. A moment later, he went in for another kiss, and the tip of her tongue snuck through to gently pry at the underside of his lips. That knocked him down like he had been shot.

Richard sat there on the ground. Spots were dancing before his eyes and ringing in his ears, not that he would call it a ringing, because the analogy was beyond his brain state at this point.

Quinn was standing over him, and Richard wasn't sure when he had got there. His two women followed after him on all fours. "Maybe I should start you off on a lower setting. Most people work their way up." Richard felt himself nodding faintly. "Okay, Settings: XIntensity:2, limitation Personal: Richard." The strange words seemed to format themselves in his mind, supplying their own syntax.

Instantly Richard's senses were back to normal, and the whole brothel felt quite a bit less dreamlike to him. The floor beneath him felt hard for the first time. He couldn't help but cast an eye towards Quinn and notice that the madame and the dark-skinned girl, who were now each slurping up and down one side of his cock, looked faintly blurry to him.

The blonde leaned forward and kissed him again, and it was still a magnificent kiss, the kind you saw in the movies but with so much more eroticism, but it was a shadow of what he had just experienced. A part of him felt empty and disappointed, but this kiss was more palatable-- he could not just stand it but return it.

He ran his hand through the blonde's silky hair, hair that felt finer and more luxurious than any could be but was at the same time real enough to fool him, to force his mind to concede that there was a woman this perfect and he was going to fuck her.

They shifted around the room in a strange dance, lips locked all the time. The blonde's tongue was sweet and her saliva was intoxicating. Their movements traveled up into the thrust of their tongues so that they were kissing with their whole bodies. She pulled him gently, and they both tumbled down to the strangely soft floor. The blonde giggled, her hair spread messily across the ground, and her expression conveying a sense of playful abandon that sent another jolt to his already-hard cock.

Her bra, or whatever it could be called, came apart easily in his hands. Richard wasn't quite prepared for her breasts. They were flawless small peaks of flesh, as full and round and pert as he could imagine, and covered by delicious soft pink nipples. He leaned down and took one in his mouth. It was every bit as sweet and addictive as her lips had been.

A naughty idea, from the recently-reactivated juvenile part of his brain, came to him. "Quinn?"

Richard turned him to see that Quinn was currently fucking Madame Lucille from behind as the black girl he had seen earlier and a strange scaly blue woman licked his balls. He wasn't sweating or panting with the exertion -- rather he was the image of virile masculine sexuality expressing its power. He looked up at Richard and answered without missing a stroke. "What is it, man?"

"Can I get another one?"

Madame Lucille, on the other hand, was only barely able to talk through her gasps of pleasure. "One of my... l-ladies... coming right up."

There was a tap on his shoulder, and Richard turned to see a vivacious and voluptuous redhead in black lingerie giving him a smoldering look. He muttered something about being good in a past life and brought her into their tangle of flesh.

The redhead's lips were just as addictive as the blonde's, but different -- a bit spicier, a bit mintier. It was, he thought in a moment of what he thought was wit, sex, and candy, just like that song that always used to get stuck in his head. The redhead lay down under him, snuggling in close to the blonde, and pulled one of his hands with her to caress her voluminous tits.

And then there was the blonde, still patiently beneath him. She looked at him with doe eyes and began gently writhing against him. It suddenly struck Richard how impossibly rude he was being -- not only breaking off in the middle of unclothing a girl to chat with another man as if she wasn't there.

And not just talk about anything, but about getting another girl to join them, with all the sympathy of ordering another shot at the bar. He would never have behaved like this before -- in real life, he had to remind himself. Of course, in real life, he would have learned the girls' names first. But this wasn't real, and they probably didn't even have names.

The touch of the redhead's tongue on his cheek ended all philosophical wanderings. He kissed her, and then kissed the blonde, reveling in the difference between their tastes. He began responding to her writhing with a steady movement of his own, practically dry humping her on the brothel floor. The redhead mounted his back and began aggressively removing (practically tearing off) his clothes. Forget about what he had thought earlier -- Richard was now sure that this was heaven.

The blonde burrowed into his newly-exposed chest, giggling and licking his muscles (which, much like Quinn's, were distinctly better than their real-life equivalents). The redhead leaned in and licked his neck as she continued to undress him with her nimble hands. He shuddered at the sensation of their warm tongues exploring his body like curious and fearless travelers.

And then the redhead tugged down his pants, and his angry red dick, having long been begging for its release, snapped free. Richard took a look at it and felt his mouth go even drier. It was a lot bigger than his real cock, and thicker. This was the stuff of pornography. It had to be at least nine inches long, he thought. But probably more. It was hard to judge in this light.

The girls seemed to be similarly entranced. They were now kneeling in front of him, looking at his cock like a just-unwrapped Christmas present. Somewhere along the line, the redhead had lost her top and her massive mounds now stood freely in the open air. For all their size, they were also incredibly firm, with dark red nipples pointing straight out. Richard reached out to feel them and was amazed at their impossible combination of softness and firmness. Taking her cue from him, the redhead reached out and began stroking his shaft, which sent a spasm of pleasure coursing through him and almost made him come right there.

The blonde timidly added her hand, placing it on the base of the shaft, and soon enough both were rubbing it in unison. Eventually, they discovered that they both needed two hands to stroke the monster. In particular, the redhead laid a hand on the very top of his dick and wrapped her palm around his cockhead, massaging it in all kinds of weird and wonderful ways. Quinn and his growing gaggle of girls were a distant memory. No, he thought. This was heaven.

But there was still another fantasy he wanted to try, and he doubted he would ever find a pair of women as obliging as these two automatons. Richard cleared his throat. "Um, could you two, you know, fuck each other?"

They grinned at the prospect. The redhead leaned in and kissed the blonde, and it was a scorcher, the kind of kiss you saw only in movies between two people passionately in love. They showed no hesitation in exploring each others' bodies, hands roaming all over. Their gasps and moans as one rolled another's nipple between her fingers or snuck her hand down under the other's last remaining underwear were downright musical. Richard found himself compelled to stroke his cock at the sight. It was better than any pornography, both in the sheer level of its beauty and the two bodies being so close to him, occasionally flicking a lusty eye to his masturbating form.

The redhead reached down and, with a strong tug, tore off the lower wrappings of the blonde before quickly dispensing with her own. Their pussies were hairless and perfectly pink. She straddled the blonde's hips and began sliding up and down on them. Their slick lower licks rubbed together, as did their soft and compliant breasts. Their moans were gentle and playful, the sound of innocents being introduced to rapture.

At first, Richard was simply entranced by the motion of their bodies, which humped with a flawless grace that real flesh could never achieve. I was like a bawdy ballet. But there was also a force of eroticism that radiated from them, a raw mass of sex strong enough to produce its gravity. And so he was drawn in. He crawled into the delta between the two girls' legs, which overlapped exactly. They both looked at him eagerly, the redhead twisting around to do so and drawing another gasp of delight from the blonde.

They were both open to him, pussies oozing with lubrication. Each promised endless pleasure, so ultimately he couldn't decide. Instead, he positioned his cock between the two girls, so that he could feel a set of warm cunt lips on each side. And with a groan, he thrust into the small sweaty gap between their bodies.

He wasn't quite fucking both of them at once, but they acted like it, crying out in delight and calling out his name. And the point between their bodies was sending him into spasms of pleasure himself. They pressed their hips together, squeezing his cock like a vice, and he promptly exploded.

It was a strange, double-bodied experience. He was at once detached from his orgasm, observing it from a distance, and entirely consumed by it, feeling an impossible level of pleasure flood his mind. This was, he was sure, better than even the best drug highs. Every inch of his flesh vibrated with joy and absolute contentment. But he was also acutely aware of the world around him, and especially the huge jets of cum that were exploding out of his oversized cock. The first burst left a pearly white trail along the girls' bodies before splashing against their busts. And then came a second, and a third, and a fourth, all equal to the first in volume and velocity. The detached part of Richard watched the hose-like performance of his virtual cock even as he could still feel the waves of ecstasy coursing through him.

He extracted himself from the two girls, who were now giggling and licking his cum off of each others' fingers. Their front sides were drenched in his emission. He was dizzy, and a little faint, but still rock hard.

"Oh yeah," said Quinn from inside a pile of female flesh. "That's another great about this program. You always stay hard."

Richard looked towards his two cum-drenched girls, staring back at him with that impossible mixture of innocence and lasciviousness, and then back down to his hard and hungry cock. He was beginning to like this world.

Kayleigh did not like their house. Or, to be more precise, her house -- she and Tom had identical units that connected through an interior door. Everything was comfortably arranged and generously lit, and it looked like a showroom model for a new suburb. The things that made a home -- the piles of clutter, the slow spread of photos and decorations, the weird gouges in the walls that each had a story behind them -- were completely absent. It felt cold and soulless.

So she stayed close to Tom, keeping one arm against his in awkward intimacy. Once again, she was startled at how quickly boredom could descend in such an unfamiliar situation. Their XP station was producing a small holographic news ticker. The items were in English, but they were incomprehensible, with all of their context unknown. It was like one of those perfectly grammatical sentences that made no sense. "Colourless green ideas sleep furiously" or something like that. She might have seen that one scrolling by between "Herrak-Iqular Trade Negotiations Break Down" and "Platero A. N. M. wins 10-B",

"You know," Tom said after a long period of staring at the flickering and floating green letters. "We could try one of those virtual reality things

Caroline was talking about. One of the educational ones, or just something for entertainment."

"Those scare me," said Kayleigh. "I like being able to tell what's real and what's not."

Tom put his arm around her. She leaned into him, more out of habit than anything else, and let her hair fall across his shirt. "Then I guess there's no avoiding the big question. What do we do with the rest of our lives? Although I have to say, it's not a new question for me."

"I still know the answer," said Kayleigh. "I'm going to be a scientist. On Earth."

Tom looked at her without his usual levity. "So you want to go home, then?"

"Of course. Don't you?"

He kissed Kayleigh on the head. "What I want doesn't matter. We're getting you home, and then I'll worry about myself. It might take a long time, and we're probably going to have to play their game for most of it. But I promise you that we'll get there."

Kayleigh felt a sudden surge of comfort. Finally, it seemed as though he understood her. He was a good guy, she thought. She couldn't remember why she had found him so dissatisfying in the past.

They lay there for a while until their clothes started melting off them.

"What the hell?" said Tom.

Kayleigh stood up and tried to deal with the phenomena of her skirt crawling down her leg and forming a puddle, which quickly rushed out of the building. "I guess those were part of Wing -- I had almost forgotten. Jeez, that gave me a start though."

When she turned around she found that Tom was looking up at her with the same reverence he always regarded her naked form with. She giggled and did a bit of a twirl. "I have to say, of all the ways of getting a girl undressed that's probably the best I've heard of."

Tom threw up his hands. "Okay, I'll admit: this was all a convoluted ploy to get into your pants. Again, I suppose."

She shook her head, her loose brown hair flowing wavelike behind her bare shoulders. Her smile took a bit of effort, as it had gotten rusty lately, but it was genuine. "You men and your tricks. Well, what else can I do?"

Kayleigh took him by the hand and dragged him to his feet. She ran a hand along her boyfriend's side. He still felt soft and warm, maybe a bit chubby, but it was a comfortable softness that she could bury herself in. His skin was a familiar territory -- she could feel the bumps and strangely isolated hairs that she knew almost instinctively now. It was something she hadn't found in Richard's arms, or Xanon's.

She continued dragging him up towards the bedroom, glancing back at him occasionally to see that cute stupefied expression he still got. As they went up the stairs, she made a show of wiggling her ass with each step. The feel of his eyes on her tickled.

Kayleigh wasn't sure whose bedroom it was -- the ownership of the identical houses seemed so arbitrary, and she couldn't remember which one they had decided to rest in. But it didn't matter. It was a soft place to fall on, spreading her naked body before Tom and taking in his nakedness as he stood in the doorway, his thick cock standing erect, his boyish features locked into a dumb grin.

She smiled at him and said, as nicely as she could manage, "What are you waiting for, big boy?"

He started at her toes. His tongue flicked out and into the gap between her big toe and the others. She couldn't help but giggle at the sensation. Tom laid butterfly kisses all over her feet, then returned to take her big toe into his mouth. The contact wasn't doing a lot for Kayleigh, but the way he looked up at her... it was worshipful. That was the only way to describe it, and she wasn't even sure if that was a word, but she didn't have time to ponder it because he was slowly moving up her legs.

Her heel, her ankle, the thin bony part of her lower leg, that strange hollow between her thigh... all lit up with the sensation of wet warmth, a sensation that was spreading through her whole body. Kayleigh leaned back and let out a moan. She felt like rubbing her breasts. More than that, she felt like grabbing Tom by the hair and shoving his face first or perhaps cock first, into her suddenly ravenous pussy. But she held off. She had to allow herself to be worshipped.

And now he was on her thigh. He seemed to take forever in planting his slow sucking kisses: first on one thigh, then the other, and then back to the first. Kayleigh moaned again, this time with more than a hint of frustration. She wanted him. He was so close to her that the top of her head kept brushing against his wetness, but he seemed to do this. Her sudden need made Kayleigh feel shocked and vulnerable, but that only made her hornier. But it was coming. It had to be. She felt its imminence, and it felt too massive to stop.

And then Tom laid his lightest kiss of all on her lower lips. Kayleigh squealed. His motions were slow and basic -- a light flick of the tongue up to her protruding clit, a fingertip wandering lazily around the rim of her cunt -- but after that taunting denial they all felt so intimate, so erotic. Kayleigh pushed herself off the mattress with her hands, trying to angle herself into his tongue. She begged for more, though looking back she couldn't remember if she used words.

Slowly he began increasing the tempo. He licked in irregular but firm circles and strokes. Perhaps, Kayleigh thought, he was writing something. If so, she felt glad to be his canvas. She pressed his head between her thighs, forming a tight triangle with her legs. Or maybe it was just to enjoy the feeling of his stubble against her skin. In any case, it only seemed to make Tom go faster and harder. Kayleigh threw her head back and howled.

Tom's tongue was marauding inside her now, lapping up her free-flowing nectar. It seemed to be everywhere at once -- simultaneously deep inside her and lovingly wrapped around her clit. Kayleigh grabbed onto her boyfriend's hair as she thrashed on the mattress, driving her pussy into his face for all she was worth. She wasn't quite sure where her orgasm began and ended, it is only a slight peak above the bliss she had already been feeling, but that strange, wet, satisfying sensation let her know that she had just come and come hard.

He was still lapping at her cunt, and the touch on that now too-sensitive part made her push his head away. "Easy boy," she said through a suddenly dry throat. "Come on up here."

"Don't need to ask me twice."

They kissed for a long while, but there was no urgency. Instead, they just lay on their sides and intertwined. It made her feel like such a pansy, but Kayleigh did like cuddling, especially the postcoital variety. It was simple human contact, and after a body-shattering experience, it made her feel whole again. There was a comfort in another person's arms that Kayleigh could never rationally understand. Must be an evolutionary trait.

But this was not quite post-coital, as the hardness jabbing into her stomach suggested. She buried her head in Tom's hair and kissed his ear. "Fuck me slowly, will you?" He didn't get a chance to respond before she grabbed his cock and guided it into her wet passage. He let out a long breath, and there they were, as together as people could be.

They didn't move, not really, for a while. Kayleigh didn't want to lose the feeling of Tom against her and didn't want to break the gaze that they were sharing. But she squeezed her legs together and did her best to clench and unclench her cunt around his cock. He had the half-pained, half-amazing expression that she knew meant pleasure. And then she felt his cock flex and swell within her, jerking upwards against her walls and her most sensitive spot, and she had to gasp. They both gave each other sly smiles. There was a rhythm to this, just like fucking, even though they were perfectly still.

But eventually, Kayleigh wanted more. She was always the one who gave in during these erotic tests of patience, even when she had just come. It was only a slight movement against him, not even a thrust, much less a hump. But he returned it, after a pause, with a bit more added. And then she brought her ass back and slid forward on his cock, enjoying the slow in-and-out. Their rhythm picked up slowly but steadily, and each new increase in speed felt like it would be the one to break her.

Their legs were hopelessly entangled, and their arms were wrapped tightly around each other, holding on for dear life, so their motion was all hips, their two bodies colliding together at one central point. Kayleigh felt his cock sliding in and out with a steady rhythm and was beginning to feel that bunching of pleasure in her nether regions, combined with pricks of pleasure all over her body. "Oh, Jesus... that feels good..."

Her second orgasm came fairly quickly. She threw herself into their mutual thrusting and let her loud feline cries flood Tom's ears. She worked her way against him, contorting around his cock. She was beginning to feel less like a beloved human being and more like an animal.

Finally, the equilibrium gave way. Tom rolled over, pinning her to the mattress. He had abandoned tenderness and was driving into her slick pussy with wild, desperate thrusts. She dug her nails into his shoulders and baited on his frantic fucking. When he came they both cried out, and a shudder passed through them as though they were one body.

Afterward, they lay intricately knotted, occasionally toying with each others' sweaty and disheveled hair. They found themselves giggling for no apparent reason. Kayleigh enjoyed the feeling of Tom's member slowly shrinking inside of her.

"I guess we should figure out the clothes situation pretty soon," said Tom.

"Probably," Kayleigh said as she nestled into the crook of his shoulder. "But can we just stay like this for a while?"

"Of course."

Richard dimly faded back into reality. He was lying on his back staring up at the perfectly even white ceiling. His body felt drained of any scrap of energy. He dimly became aware of his real physical form, sweat-drenched and weak compared to the virtual casanova he had just inhabited for -- how long had it been? Hours? Days? But there was no sign of stickiness around his crotch, or even hardness, from his copious and voluminous ejaculations.

Quinn was sitting up, his recovery faster than Richard's. "So what did you think?"

Richard managed to get sound through his mothballed throat. "I... I've never experienced anything like that. It was amazing. Just... an absolute sensation." It was, Richard thought, hedonism taken to its ultimate end. You couldn't improve on it, only change its focus.

"And to think that you were only at double strength," said Quinn. "There's an exciting world ahead of you, my friend. You'll never want to touch a meatspace girl again."

"I don't know," said Richard. "I mean, real girls... it's different. It's another mind you can interact with, not just a set of orifices. Not that the orifices aren't great and all."

"You want a name? Conversation? A personality? A backstory? I've got the chip. There are a lot more complex scenarios, believe me. I just like to cut to the chase, personally."

Richard was too tired to pretend that he wasn't intrigued. After all, wasn't the pornography of an alien world as fascinating a subject as its geography? He should take in all the information he could. For science.

Quinn perched over him, grinning. "I've got some friends I think you should meet."

Chapter: 5

The creatures could almost be mistaken for squid, were it not for the scrabbling claws that hung out of their gelatinous body where tentacles would be, as well as their evident comfort on dry land. Kayleigh watched in a mixture of horror and fascination as they scrambled across the floor, making little scritch-scratch sounds, and balanced plates of food on their head. Of course, most of the clientele of the restaurant were the same species, sitting comfortably at the low tables that the humans had to kneel at. For the fifth time that day, Kayleigh was sure she was in a dream.

"What did you say these creatures were called again?" she said.

Mona took a sip of some blue liquid that had been served in square cups (or maybe they were bowls). "Kowlai. At least that's the closest human phonetic approximation. They're like us, you know -- their planet isn't part of the League yet, but they got scooped up for seeing too much. Lovely species -- they make beautiful music; you should hear it. And just wait until you taste the tinita. It's fabulous."

Kayleigh nodded weakly. Mona had been taking them on the grand tour, showing them all the sights of their tower, which hosted any number of diasporic species. They had passed through a warehouse floor that resembled a department store in every way but the Muzak, and a floor that was nothing but a wide-open field for sports and recreation. It was hard to even think of them as floors, given how closely they mimicked the outdoors. When they had stepped off on the kowlai floor it had seemed equally external, but with a massive lake in the Centre of it, and two small but fierce red suns hanging in the sky, casting a crimson pallor across everything.

Tom lifted the cup bowl to his lips and took a deep sip of the blue liquid. He nodded and gave Kayleigh the thumbs-up she didn't know she had been waiting for. She took a sip of it herself. It had a bit of the feel of tea, but it also tasted a bit like a meaty soup. It was a strange, thick concoction, but she found herself drinking it again.

Their waiter (and it felt weird to apply such a normal term to the kowlai) scrambled over to their table, a full tray of food cushioned safely by his bulbous head. Mona lifted the three identical plates off the tray and put one in front of each of them. Kayleigh couldn't help but stare at the glint of Mona's robotic arm, but the meal soon captured her attention. The gray meat sat in a deep blue sauce with flecks of some mysterious red substance in it. It didn't look that appetizing, but it did smell nice.

"I guess we know where they've been keeping the blue food," said Tom.

With more than a bit of trepidation, Kayleigh took the (fairly normal) eating utensils and sawed herself off a bit of the tinita meat. It oozed black bile as she tore away a section of the fleshy membrane.

"Go on," said Mona. "Try it."

Kayleigh put it into her mouth and it was, of course, amazing. She let the strange juices pool on her tongue, enjoying their play of sweetness and salt and devoured the gooey meat.

"Wait, what did you say this was again?" she said.

"Tinita," Mona said. "A big fish native to Kowlai that they've managed to capture and grow here. These are its intestines -- but that's the best part, you know."

Kayleigh shrugged, deciding to roll with the strangeness this time. Hey, if alien fish intestines tasted this good, she would eat them. Tom seemed to have come to the same conclusion, and was ripping apart his tinita.

Mona smiled. "See, this is what I've been saying. So many people see coming here as a loss or a trauma, but I like to think of it as an opportunity to experience new things. It's a big universe out there, and there's so much to try." Tom nodded eagerly.

"The question is," said Kayleigh. "How do we get out there to see it? Right now we seem to be cooped up in this huge building."

"No reason to think of yourself as 'cooped up'" said Mona. "Honestly, I don't even think about going outside anymore -- or I suppose it's that I think of our courtyard as being 'outside', even though technically it's inside, but they do a good job at making you forget it. If that makes any sense. Honestly, even if you go on vacation to another planet, you'll still probably be indoors most of the time. The universe wasn't made for humans to gallivant around all of it, you know. Lots of weird gases and chemicals that we gotta avoid."

"Weird chemicals can be fun sometimes," Tom said, in between scoops of the fragrant tinita juice.

There had been a question sitting on Kayleigh's chest for the whole dinner and she decided to finally come out with it. "So Mona. When I was on Earth I was a graduate student. Now, I know that my knowledge is going to seem very provincial or outdated or just plain wrong over here. I guess my question is... how do I sign up to learn what I was missing? I mean, do you even have schools over here?"

Mona laughed. "We have schools over here. Two buildings down are the New University -- they have classes for all sorts of diasporic species. You can also get vids from the Central Academy on any topic, you can think of, from toddler-level education up to stuff that only geniuses can start to understand. Of course, language is also an issue. There aren't degrees or anything like that -- people just take the classes that they want."

Kayleigh wrinkled her nose. She had hoped that maybe she could settle into her old routine here, a routine that she never realized she had been so attached to, but it would be impossible to obtain that same status here. Oh well. New opportunities, new knowledge. Wasn't that what science was about? She tried to force herself to stay open-minded.

"Of course," said Mona. "We're going to have to get some information from you guys too. Just a standard debriefing -- tell the authorities what you know about your world, what's changed since the last update on Earth, and what wasn't covered by previous adaptees. Who knows, maybe they'll decide Earth has developed to a point where they can be admitted into the League of Worlds."

"Isn't this League or whatever it is monitoring Earth?" said Kayleigh. "I mean, that's how we got picked up."

"Our activities around there have been minimal for a couple of decacycles," said Mona. "And in any case, we weren't there to gather information on your culture -- we were there to make sure that nothing interfered with a crucial stage in your species's development. Truth be told, most researchers have lost interest in Earth recently. It's just another self-destructive backwater planet now. I mean, no offense or anything." Mona covered her mouth as if she had said too much, yet again.

Kayleigh wondered what had made Mona think of this alien society -- the League of Worlds -- as "we", and think of her own species as some distant unrelated race. But maybe with all her cybernetic enhancements, Mona wasn't that human anymore.

"Well," said Tom, scraping up the last parts of his tinita. "That was delicious. We have to come by this place with Richard sometime."

Mona frowned at the mention of their companion. "I wish he could have joined us on this expedition. I wonder what he could be busy with, so soon after arriving."

Wing had claimed that the street-level environment was ideal for human habitation, but to Richard, it looked a lot like a slum. A shantytown of shops and stalls ran through the streets, curling around the monolithic buildings that stretched up further than the eye could see. Creatures of all races yelled, stomped, waved tentacles, and let loose rancid burps to hawk their disreputable-looking wares. Shady characters darted in and out of narrow corners, and at one point a billow of purplish smoke made his eyes sting to the point where he worried he might go blind.

Up ahead, Quinn was weaving through the crowd with a grace that betrayed his flabby body. Richard tried to follow him but jostled and bumped into three different aliens with every step. "Sorry," he apologized to a hissing lizard creature. If Quinn didn't stand out so much, both for his clammy gray skin and is one of the few humans in sight, Richard might worry about losing him.

He sighed and muttered under his breath. "Why did I agree to come out here?"

Of course, he knew the reason: his idyllic, quasi-suburban home in the artificial village they called Madrid had already become stifling and dull. It was like a hotel room, oppressive in its bland comfort. He had immersed himself in the XP device and its virtual world for a couple of days, but it was hard to know where to start there. With the dramas and comedies, some of which the viewer was a mere audience for, others which put the viewer in the center of the action and had the world react to their actions? With education, the thousands of lectures and courses in hundreds of disciplines, many of which were completely unknown to him? With the simple nature simulations that let him wander the wilds of an alien planet unimpeded? With the copious pornography, in which every species, gender, act, and relationship was represented? Or maybe the simulators of food and drink, which surpassed any dining experience Richard had had on Earth (as well as the bland, government-produced meals he had found his strange cubic refrigerator stocked with?) It was the kind of wealth of riches that left one paralyzed. He needed to go out, and experience real life, and that was what Quinn promised.

Quinn waved to him from further up in the crowd, his pinched face twisted in impatience. "Come on! Just shove your way through!"

Richard lead with his shoulder and managed to cleave through the throng a bit, but once he ran into a big alien whose skin looked like it was made of rock he decided that politeness might be the way to go. He did eventually make his way to Quinn, who had stopped in the middle of the block and was tapping his feet in a very irritating manner.

"First rule of the undercity," said Quinn. "When you're walking, you gotta be an asshole."

"I'll keep that in mind," said Richard. "Are we here?"

Quinn gestured down a set of steps running off the street to what looked like any subterranean, hole-in-the-wall bar you might find on Earth. A pang of nostalgia hit Richard. "Big Jill's Watering Hole" was written on the door in English, several other human languages, and some strange (probably alien) alphabets that Richard didn't know.

Inside the bar the lighting was low and the mood lower. Two despondent-looking human men were playing pool over by one corner, while a small group of shady characters was gathered in a booth in another corner. A tank of a woman -- Big Jill, presumably -- sat behind the bar, drying a glass while she idly looked out onto the patrons. Two aliens with heavily ridged heads and four sets of arms were talking in low tones at the bar.

"Welcome to my home away from home," said Quinn. "It ain't much, I know, but--"

"It's perfect," Richard said.

Quinn took him to the group in the corner, who greeted him like an old friend. "Hi, all," said Quinn. "This is Richard. He just got beamed down next to me. Don't worry, he's a good guy, y'know." The rest of the table let out a collective grumble that might have been a greeting.

A skinny, greasy kid brushed his hair out of his eyes and spoke. "So Quinn, have you heard the latest?"

"About the mining rig on Apellis-5?" Quinn snorted. "I always knew those things were a disaster waiting to happen. And now half of a moon's up in flames."

"Unsound design," muttered a heavily-bearded man at the other end of the table.

"Wait, what is this?" said Richard.

A woman with spiky blue hair snorted. "Of course, why would anyone care about what's going on in the world? It doesn't matter what the League is doing light-years away. It doesn't matter what's going on two floors down. We can just sit in our cocoons and bask in all the banal little pleasures they see fit to dispense to us."

Richard was vaguely offended, and not sure what he had done to be the target of the woman's vitriol. "Sorry, I just got here. So, you don't like the League?"

"No," said the woman. "I don't like the League. I don't like a nice benevolent daddy figure deciding everything for me. I don't like technology that removes us from reality or buildings that remove us from nature. Most of all, I don't like having not seen my family for thirty years because they still think Earth is too goddamn primitive and barbaric."

"Don't mind Shelley," said Quinn. "She's... opinionated. Obnoxious, even." He turned to the woman in question. "Take it easy on the savvie here, okay?"

Shelley gave Quinn the middle finger. "Blow it out your asshole, Quinn."

Richard took a closer look at Shelley. Her punky, spiked-blue hair was complemented by a ragged outfit full of holes and patches. If she weren't older than him, she would have fit in at any deafeningly-loud concert of teenage rebellion. Her body had the hints of middle-aged flab, but for the most part, when he looked at her he just saw a nice figure and a personality he couldn't help but be drawn to.

"The fuck are you staring at?" said Shelley.

"Oh, nothing," said Richard. "It's just... it's good to meet new people."

Shelley shrugged and sipped her beer. "Fucking weirdo," she said, none too quietly.

Tom had been absorbed in the XP machine all day. Kayleigh had taken a look at it, but re-educating herself seemed like such an immense undertaking that she was afraid to get started. On the other hand, Tom had dove right into it and was becoming something of an addict. It was a little irritating if she was being honest.

She sat for a little while on the couch, looking at Tom's blank expression. He looked a bit like a monk, sitting cross-legged on the floor and staring serenely at nothing. He also looked like he had all those times she had come home to find him vegetating in front of some decades-old Star Trek episode, having spent another unambitious day on the couch.

Kayleigh thought about disturbing him but ultimately decided to leave him to his bliss. She went out the front door and sat on the stoop. The houses of Madrid ringed an emerald-green lawn, every blade of grass evenly and meticulously cut. On the other side of the lawn a family was playing, a small red ball being tossed between father and son, enacting the oldest rituals on this far-off planet. It was disgustingly picturesque.

She went next door and knocked. It only took a moment for Caroline to open the door, beaming and giggly. "Hiya, Kayleigh. How's it going?"

"It's going... okay." Kayleigh wished she could have Caroline's energy and seemingly bottomless cheer. "I was just a little sick of hanging around that house. You doing anything interesting?"

"Oh, I never do anything interesting," said Caroline. "But you can come inside anyway."

Caroline and Esh's house had the same layout as Kayleigh's, but the walls were plastered with decorations. Kayleigh stopped and fixated on a watercolor painting of an older woman with long, elegant silver hair and, next to it, a harsh mask encrusted with yellow jewels.

"This is Esh's and my art," said Caroline. "I do the painting -- that's my mother, back on Earth. The mask is Esh's -- apparently, that's a major art form back in his home world. He says it's a portrait of me. I don't see it, myself, but I guess the lack of a beak should give it away."

They moved into the living room. Kayleigh sat down on a comfortable divan that sank beneath her weight. "You want some wine?" said Caroline.

"You have wine here?" said Kayleigh. It was the best news she had heard in weeks.

"Well, not actual wine, if you want to get technical," said Caroline. "Rafael from the other side of the floor makes it. There's a plant on some planet named Orexis that is really close to the Earth's grape. Close enough for government work, as my dad always said." Caroline produced an unmarked bottle of sparkling white liquid from a cabinet in the corner. It looked like wine and, as Kayleigh quickly discovered, it sure tasted like wine.

"So what's Tom up to right now?" said Caroline as she took her first sip.

"Oh, no doubt he's immersed in some interesting VR thing," said Kayleigh.

"And you couldn't drag him away?"

Kayleigh hesitated. She feared that airing out her complaints would just make her seem petty. "I dunno, I shouldn't bitch..."

"Hey, bitch away," said Caroline, raising her glass into the air in a weird kind of toast. "I wanna hear the dirt. Do people still say that on Earth? The dirt?"

Maybe it was the wine, but Kayleigh was shocked to fall so easily into conversation with Caroline. They talked about stupid gossip and shared fond memories of teenage slumber parties. Caroline tried to explain art to Kayleigh, which was somewhat more successful than when Kayleigh tried to explain science to Caroline. Another glass down, Caroline confided in the terror she had felt when she first came here, and how much Esh had helped her come to terms with the new world. Kayleigh put a comforting arm around her shoulder. And then they moved onto lighter topics, remembering cheesy movies from old Earth. For a fleeting moment, Kayleigh let herself forget where she was and everything that had happened, and fell into a more comfortable rhythm.

The door pushed open and Caroline sprang to her feet. "Esh!" The bird alien soberly calmly walked into the hallway and looked at the two women. Kayleigh tried to read the emotion in his beady black eyes but found it impossible. Caroline threw her arms around Esh.

"I and Kayleigh were just getting caught up," said Caroline. Esh said something in his rhythmic language. Caroline giggled. "Yeah, we were bad. Hey, the wine doesn't do anything for you anyways."

Esh responded, prompting more giggling. "Here, come sit down with us."

Kayleigh wasn't sure if Esh even could sit down, but he did a close enough approximation by squatting town on his three legs (or maybe they were talons) until his butt touched the ground.

He did look sort of ridiculous when he did it, though. Kayleigh was suddenly aware of his sheer bulk, his physical presence so close to hers. She could see the spots on his otherwise pristine white feathers, and smell his strangely citrusy odor. Caroline sat down beside her, much closer than before, shoulder to shoulder, her warm stomach pressing uncomfortably against Kayleigh's side.

"Hey," Kayleigh said. "You know, I'm sorry if I acted like a bitch the last time you saw me. I was just you know... upset." She couldn't help breaking out in laughter. Why was she laughing?

Esh said something, and Caroline translated by whispering breathily into Kayleigh's ear. "Esh says it's alright. He's heard much worse." Kayleigh wasn't sure why Caroline was whispering now, but it felt just fine.

"So, um, how was your day at work?" said Kayleigh.

"He wasn't at work. He was out flying," said Caroline. "Lousy polluted air out there, so it's not good for it... well, at least that's what Esh says. But he needs to stretch his wings, you know? Well, I guess you don't know, but you know the feeling, or at least I do. And besides which, it always gets him in the mood." More of her infectious giggling.

Kayleigh swallowed. She noticed for the first time a firmness poking out of Esh's bundle of red sashes, making a small tent. "I can get out of here if you guys want."

Caroline rubbed her cheek against Kayleigh's. "Stay." Maybe it was just the wine, but Kayleigh had a hard time finding a reason not to.

As Kayleigh drained the last ounces from her glass Caroline pressed herself against her alien boyfriend, rubbing her hand in big circles across his right flank. She leaned in and kissed the spot underneath his wing, provoking a throaty cry that Kayleigh was pretty sure with pleasure. Kayleigh realized that her mouth was dry and that she absolutely couldn't look away.

"Come on," said Caroline. "Have a touch."

Kayleigh got to her feet and slowly walked towards Esh as if in a trance. She ran her hand along the feathers of his left wing, feeling their smooth texture. From up close he looked so majestic. When Esh stretched out his wing and tucked Kayleigh inside of it, she was amazed at the raw physicality of this ungainly creature. She ran her fingers through the short yellow fur of Esh's insides, feeling the incredible warmth that came from him. He had put his other wing around Caroline in the same fashion, and she was unashamedly nuzzling up to her lover and kissing his strange anatomy.

"There are about six female dendra to every male," said Caroline in between kisses. "Esh here is used to the idea of having a harem. I imagine he's felt quite unfulfilled with just little old me to pleasure him. But now things are looking up..."

With that, Caroline tugged at the knot of sashes around Esh's waist and let what passed for his clothing fall away. Kayleigh's eyes bugged out at the size of his cock. It was a pale yellow, the same color as the feathers that surrounded it, and it maintained the same girth all the way through, with no bulbous head or notable ridges. And it had to be at least a foot long.

"Jesus," said Kayleigh as she continued to stare at the alien phallus.

"I know, right?" said Caroline with a hint of smugness. She tugged her blouse over her head and tossed it casually aside. Her clamshell bra soon joined it. Kayleigh couldn't help but stare at the other woman's thin torso and her petite, pert breasts, topped with joyful pink nipples. She hadn't realized before how beautiful Caroline was. Her hair, the color of the insides of strawberries, fell around her shoulders and cast an aura of fiery luminescence around her.

Caroline fell to her knees and began running her hand along Esh's cock. Esh made another one of those throaty noises in response, and Kayleigh could feel it passing through her, making her shudder and shiver as she pressed herself closer to his bulk. She tentatively reached out a hand and ran it along the hard black surface of his legs, never taking her eyes off the strange sight of Caroline enthusiastically jacking him off.

"Come here," said Caroline. "You try."

Kayleigh joined her friend on her knees in front of Esh's long penis. Up close, it looked almost dangerous in its size, but she felt a strange compulsion to touch it. And so touch it she did, at first lightly running her fingertips along its rubber-like surface, and then wrapping her fist around it and giving an experimental pump. Esh gave a coo of approval. She started stroking his cock slowly and lovingly. When a drop of precum appeared at the tip, she spread it around the glans and rubbed it into the skin in the way she remembered guys always liking. Kayleigh didn't know much about dendra anatomy, but if she was interpreting Esh's increasingly throaty cries right, she was doing a good enough job.

When Kayleigh had cheated in the past, with Richard and Xanon, it felt like she was sliding into a dark inevitability. But this was different. Maybe it was just the wine, but she felt incredibly free and saw no reason why she shouldn't reach out and grab that freedom by the hand -- or the cock, as it were. Instead of darkness, she was in a field of light.

She looked over at Caroline's beautiful breasts and realized that she was wearing too much clothing. So Kayleigh let go of Esh's cock and pulled her shirt over her head. Caroline quickly picked up the slack, lowering her head to her lover's crotch and sucking his dick into her mouth. Kayleigh watched with rapt fascination as Caroline's head bobbed up and down on the alien cock, her red hair bouncing behind her. Kayleigh found herself leaning in closer and closer.

Caroline released Esh's cock from her mouth and turned to Kayleigh, who had just now realized how close the two girls were to each other. And then they were kissing -- Kayleigh wasn't sure who had closed the little distance between them. Caroline's lips were urgent and passionate and tasted a bit of lemon. Kayleigh had never touched another woman intimately before, never had had more than idle thoughts about it, but here it just felt like another good idea. The next thing she knew, Caroline's arms were wrapped around her neck and her hands were fondling Caroline's breasts, which were fascinating in their slight difference from her own.

Esh cooed, and Caroline broke from Kayleigh with a bit of an embarrassed smile on her face. "I think he wants some attention." She jerked her head towards Esh's swollen cock, already slick with her saliva.

Kayleigh leaned in to take Esh in her mouth. As she got even closer his cock seemed even bigger, a pulsing pillar of masculinity. But she could at least fit a little bit in her mouth. And then a bit more. And then she managed to get halfway down the monstrous organ before the tip was butting the edge of her throat.

Using well-practiced skills, Kayleigh began bobbing up and down on Esh's cock. She kept her lips tightly pressed to his skin so that he could feel their soft strokes as they traversed the length of his dick. She swirled her tongue around his smooth length, creating a smorgasbord of sensation that she knew no man -- human or otherwise -- could resist.

"He's gonna come," Caroline said, giggly. Kayleigh released Esh from her mouth with a pop. She and Caroline both wrapped a hand around Esh's phallus and stroked up and down in tandem, looking up at him expectantly. With a shrill cry that startled Kayleigh, he began spurting from his cock.

It wasn't like human ejaculate -- it was translucent and had the scent and texture of an uncooked egg white. And it was much more copious than any human man's orgasm. Kayleigh felt the first gush land across her face before Caroline jerked Esh's cock over towards her and let him paint her tits with his strange seed. It looked so nice that Kayleigh made sure her chest was the recipient of his next torrent, the biggest one yet. She felt as though she had been splattered with a bucket of the stuff, covering her in a warm gooey layer. Caroline ended up with the next spurt in her hair, and another blast of ejaculation sprayed onto the carpet. Esh shuddered to a stop, as what remained of his cum poured out of his cock as though it was a faucet.

"Holy shit," said Kayleigh.

"I know, right?" said Caroline. "I go through a lot of dry-cleaning. You should feel him go off inside you! It's like fucking a fire hose. Er, in a good way."

Kayleigh looked down at her torso, splattered in dendra cum. "How are we going to get all of this off."

"I have an idea." Caroline leaned down and, with a naughty smile on her face, licked a small patch of cum off Kayleigh.

The two girls got thoroughly clean.

Tom had unplugged himself from the XP system an hour ago and had spent the time since laying on the couch, trying to take it all in. There was just so much out there. Hundreds, if not thousands of species, each with as much history, art, and life as humans. He had spent the day climbing the galaxy's largest volcano, riding an insectoid alien through the Vultari deserts, and getting a fly-on-the-wall's view of the founding of the Galactic Federation. Real life was a bit of a disappointment after that, even a real-life as strange as the one he was now immersed in.

Kayleigh came in, humming. She looked positively refreshed, and Tom wondered if there were health spas on this planet. "What were you up to?"

"Oh, not much. Just visiting the neighbors."

Tom smiled. "It's good to see you happy. I was worried you were going to sulk in your room until the end of time."

"Well, it's good to be happy." Kayleigh leaned in and kissed him. She tasted strange -- a little citrusy. And wafting around her shoulders was the distinct scent of an egg.

THE END

OTHER BOOKS BY THE AUTHOR

Karmic Love

Undercover

Eternal Love

Undying Lust

The Good Taste

Offence and Justice

A Model for Murder

Lethal Legacy

Lethal Legacy 2

Paranormal Club

Enchanted Souls

Beginners of Nowhere

Wildflower

Mystic Agent

Dark Angel

Lonesome Moonlight

The Eerie Egg

A Romantic Crime

www.ingramcontent.com/pod-product-compliance
Lightning Source LLC
Chambersburg PA
CBHW070500170726
48291CB00008B/2580